Matilda Betham-Edwards

Next of Kin Wanted

Vol. II

Matilda Betham-Edwards

Next of Kin Wanted
Vol. II

ISBN/EAN: 9783337066536

Printed in Europe, USA, Canada, Australia, Japan

Cover: Foto ©Andreas Hilbeck / pixelio.de

More available books at **www.hansebooks.com**

NEXT OF KIN WANTED.

A Novel.

BY

M. BETHAM-EDWARDS,

AUTHOR OF 'KITTY,' 'DR. JACOB,' 'HALF-WAY,' ETC.

IN TWO VOLUMES.

VOL. II.

LONDON:

RICHARD BENTLEY AND SON,

Publishers in Ordinary to Her Majesty the Queen.

1887.

CONTENTS OF VOL. II.

NEXT OF KIN—WANTED.

CHAPTER I.

MRS. DE ROBERT HOLDS FORTH ON RELATIONS.

NEITHER Briardale nor Hopedale can be called show-places, yet fewer spots in England have more quiet beauty to show. Nowhere is it easier to find delicious nooks and woodland scenes that seem to have been created expressly for happy holiday folks. Briardale itself is so beautiful and romantic, that but for church, post-office, and trim cottages, lovers of the picturesque could not do better than picnic in the village street ! On either side are breezy bits of moor-

land, coppice, leafy woods, and cool pastures,
inviting to solitude and repose. Within a
stone's-throw of the village, the stranger is as
well off as in the forest of Arden; whilst the
prospect from the upper part is one of the
fairest in England.

Morecambe Bay is beautiful at all times,
alike in high-tide, when it shows a vast sheet
of silvery water; or when, completely drained,
nothing but a brown velvety expanse of
smoothest sand meets the eye. And exquisite
the frame of such a picture: rich hanging
woods on one side, near enough to show the
intermingled hues of oak, beech, and syca-
more; on the other, the receding hills, gold
and violet at dawn and sunset, a pale azure
cloud in noonday glare.

In a sweet spot commanding this view,
Miss Ivory next day was doing woodland
honours. She had marshalled her little
company to a grassy platform not far from the
village, whence, in cool shadow all the while,
they could behold the vast sun-bright picture.

Sabina and Prue, on the Curate's behalf, were to provide tea; and the Vicar, by way of testifying the sincerity of his forgiveness, had promised to partake. Mr. Bacchus, meantime, was on no account whatever to allude to what had happened.

'You must understand,' Mr. Meridian said to Eugenia beforehand, 'it never was, and never could be, my intention to quarrel with Bacchus. What, in heaven's name, have we to quarrel about? But if I yet find myself obliged to administer the sharpest rebuke he has ever incurred in his life, the fault will be his own.'

She had too much faith in the Vicar's self-control, and the Curate's remorse, to dread another encounter. And as yet, although the afternoon advanced, neither Vicar nor Curate appeared.

Meantime, the little company was in the highest spirits. Seated in a semicircle on the mossy ground, each entertained by turns.

'How well we all get on together!' said Mrs. de Robert, addressing herself to the supposed missionary; 'and shall I tell you why? It is because we are not relations.'

Sabina and Prue blushed with a look of downright guilt ; the priest and the Americans looked at Miss Ivory and each other, unable to resist a smile. The Doctor was the first to take up the gauntlet.

'Prove to me, my dear madam, that we are not one and all descendants from Adam and Eve, and I accept your proposition. But is not humanity composed of cousins many times removed? Relationship I take to be like those strong essences concocted by pharmacy. A drop chokes and consumes us—a mild dilution is swallowed with pleasure. Who ever heard of a man murdering his father's brother's wife's sister's son's mother-in-law, while parricide and matricide are common. No, Mrs. de Robert is right ; we can live in peace and angelic harmony with everybody in the world, keeping murderous hands alike off saint and demon— provided they are neither our next of kin nor heirs at law.'

'Pretty morality that!' retorted the elder Derrober. 'You ought to blush as red as a poppy for uttering it. What will this gentleman, a minister of religion, have to say to you? For my part, I accept your first position, and stop there. Kinsfolk we all are, and kinsfolk we must remain. But, heaven be praised! no law compels us to herd together like a flock of sheep. We may choose as boon companions and sworn friends those of our blood and name who are so much in sympathy with us as to seem our second selves.'

Mrs. de Robert smiled grimly. The missionary entered on the lists in mild, bland tones.

'A profoundly interesting and not easily exhausted theme,' he said, 'and one in which priest and layman must naturally differ. In our eyes, consanguinity holds a second place, and affinity in matters of faith is all in all. Were every member of the present company related to me, it would be my duty to love one and all. Are they fellow-worshippers at the same shrine, then are they beloved brethren and sisters, although bound by no tie of blood.'

'That is how you missionaries feel, of course,' Mrs. de Robert said, 'and if not, poor heathen folk would never have been induced to wear clothes and give up eating each other. I always put half a sovereign in the missionary plate myself.'

'Ah!' broke in the elder Derrober, his face lighting up with enthusiasm. 'Let us beware of tumbling headlong into a pitfall! Does not the sublime sentiment of relationship lie deeper than our reverend friend would have us believe ? To be kindly affectioned towards those who agree with us in religion—that is to say, in everything—is no hard task. But to love those who swear by the Koran instead of our own Bible ; who worship Auguste Comte instead of the Virgin Mary ; who go to a Swedenborgian chapel on Sundays whilst the rest of us are streaming into the parish church—there, methinks, lies the gist of the matter !'

'For my part,' added the Doctor, 'I am

never better pleased than when I see people
hustling each other about for the sake of
religion. It proves that we are not high-class
apes anyhow, as Darwin tries to make out.
No, sir,' he said, turning to the so-called missionary; 'you are right, and that old gentleman yonder, my uncle, is wrong. There will
be no more fine doings in the world till the
age of religious persecution begins anew, and
all who get the chance burn their neighbours
for calling their souls their own. But the
ladies—have they not a word to say, either
for their relations or their religion ?'

'Suppose they have neither one nor the
other ?' Mrs. de Robert said provokingly.
She delighted in nothing so much as shocking
people by little reckless speeches that often
meant nothing.

Sabina remained dumb. Prue felt bound
to come forward on behalf of the black coat
and theology. She might affront her rough
kinswoman, with grave consequences to herself. She could not help it. She was one of
those women who ought to have lived in the

Middle Ages, or at least had something like a chance in the way of martyrdom.

'I don't think,' she began, with a little blush of excitement, 'that one need be very learned to see the right and wrong in these matters. We have only to think of Eve and the apple, and everything becomes as clear as possible. Had Eve been a right-minded woman and a dutiful wife, we should all be of one opinion about religion, and love each other whether relations or no, of course.'

'I doubt if we should be much the better for that,' Mrs. de Robert jerked out. 'However, no one is readier to love their relations than I am, if I could only find them out. Would you believe it,' she said, looking at the three men, 'I am in the veriest quandary ever heard of! I want folks who can prove themselves kith and kin—my husband's, I mean; and though I have spent upwards of fifty pounds on advertisements and inquiries of all kinds, nobody turns up.'

'Then,' said the elder Derrober, with an insinuating smile, 'there is nothing left for

you to do but adopt ideal kinsfolk, men and
women after your own heart.'

'One thing is quite certain,' put in the
Doctor : 'adoption would make a man of me,
morally, spiritually, socially. I am in the
position of an ill-fated peach. The sun has
ripened it, the breeze has sent it tumbling
to earth; but there it lies, no one to pick
it up.'

'I might do worse,' Mrs. de Robert said.
'You are vastly entertaining.'

'Pay no heed, I entreat you, madam,' said
the elder, 'to this scapegrace, this good-for-
nothing, this devil-me-care ! If you want no
fair-weather concern, but a taut ship that will
ride to port through a dozen gales, take me.
If adoption is sweet to the young, the
lusty, and the hopeful, how much more so
must it be to those in the sere and yellow
leaf ! Adoption, if carried out in a proper
spirit, offers a solution of the gravest problems
that perplex philosophers. Were one half of
humanity to adopt the other half, philanthropy would have said its last word, and

this terrestrial globe would once more enjoy a golden age.'

'Nay,' began the missionary in clear silvery tones, and smiling as he spoke. 'Beware, madam, of these unbashful materialists, these transparent sceptics. Rome, it is true, availed herself of the divine principle of adoption. The Church and the Church alone has carried out its true spirit. The aim of Rome was to strengthen her dread empire, and knit in closer bands citizen with citizen. The Church has set herself to diminish orphanhood, to shelter the helpless! So,' here he turned once more to Mrs. de Robert with an engaging smile, 'adopt me—in other words, the Church—and you become at once the feeder of the hungry, the clother of the naked, the teacher of the ignorant—a nameless Providence to thousands!'

'I have not a single word to say against any one of you,' was the good-natured reply. 'I have not, indeed. I'd as lief see my poor husband's property in your hands as in any other. Only, you see, you do not possess the necessary qualifications. You don't belong to the family.'

Miss Ivory looked delightfully provocative. Sabina and Prue could not conceal an expression of embarrassment. The three men remained perfectly cool.

'Have we ever said so ?' the Doctor began. 'You never asked us, that I know of. Now I just ask you to eye that old gentleman, my uncle, yonder. Did you ever see a hungrier, more lanthorn-jawed face; a more shark-like look ? Blanket him like Sancho Panza, and you'll never hear two gold pieces chinking in his pockets, I'll warrant you. Then look at me—yes, look at me, madam. Don't hurry. Take your time. What on earth should I be roving about the world for, at my age, a bachelor, ready for anything that turns up ? Of course, like my uncle, I'm some poor relation waiting to be adopted. I couldn't be otherwise. Then cast your eyes upon the reverend gentleman sitting next you. You must know what he is sniffing in the wind !

When did a parson lose the chance of pocketing a little money ?'

Mrs. de Robert seemed to relish the joke keenly.   She thought it the best possible.

' Well,' she said, ' produce your credentials. Out with your pedigrees, and you shall have anything you like—that I have to give, I mean.'

The Doctor rubbed his hands with a look of exultation.

' You hear that, uncle ? But, my dear madam, you cannot be serious. Supposing we could all three do this—my uncle, the reverend gentleman sitting next you, and myself. Supposing, I say, we could prove to your satisfaction that we come of the true de Robert stock, would you give us so much as a dollar apiece ? Bestow money on a couple of adventurers from the other side of the Atlantic —revolutionaries, dynamiters, for aught you know, in disguise ? Fill the pockets of a missionary, corrupter of the innocent heathen ; foister of civilization and the gin-bottle upon ingenuous Arcadians beyond seas ? No, you would not—you could not, consistently with sanity, enrich such a set.'

'What folks would do with the money when they get it is no concern of mine,' Mrs. de Robert said. 'My duty is to find the rightful owners; and I shall do my duty.'

'There speaks one I am proud to claim as my kinswoman!' said the elder Derrober, carried away by his enthusiasm. 'Madam, I will no longer conceal the truth. You see before you three descendants of that noble de Robert who sacrificed himself for his country on Bosworth Field.'

'Then I will never speak to any one of you again!' cried Mrs. de Robert, exasperated beyond measure.

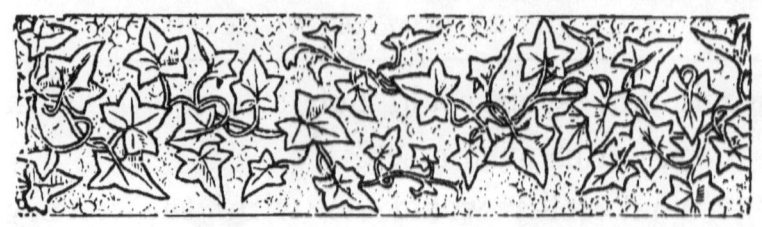

CHAPTER II.

THE WOLVES UNMASKED.

SHE did, however, speak to them again, and to some purpose. The cup of ire was full to the brim. It must perforce overflow. Meantime Miss Ivory, calmness itself, waited, to pour oil on the troubled waters, till the first fury of the storm should have somewhat abated. Sabina and Prue looked the very images of vexation. They had not enjoyed so many gala days in the course of their existence that they could afford to see this one spoiled.

The behaviour of the delinquents was characteristic. The incorrigible Doctor evidently enjoyed the situation. His uncle wore an

expression of almost apostolic self-reproach
and resignation. As to the missionary—in
other words, the Jesuit father—his behaviour
was exactly what might have been expected
from him from first to last, that of the finished
gentleman, the amiable savant, and the con-
summate man of the world.

'To think,' began Mrs. de Robert, first of
all addressing herself to the elder Derrober,
'that a man of your years, a Christian as •I
suppose you term yourself, and a citizen of
the finest country in the world—I say, that you
should demean yourself by playing tricks like
a schoolboy, shaming your gray hairs by
taking in an old woman like me, cajoling and
carrying for the sake of filthy lucre. When
I say a thing I mean it. When I advertised
for my late husband's next of kin, I wished to
find 'em. And when I said they were wanted
for something to their advantage, I spoke the
truth. Why could you not be square, give
me an honest tit for tat, say your say and
have done ? It was not my business to
praise you up to the skies or pick you to

pieces. All I had to do was to find out whether you were the right people or no, and act accordingly. My husband's people may be the veriest riffraff that ever were, the tag-rag and bobtail of society, the scum of the earth, or angels dropped from heaven—'tis no sort of business of mine. What made you suppose I was not a woman of my word? Ah! I should like to know that. You'll have to throw a little light on the matter before you have done, I can tell you.'

The victim of this castigation remained mute, as if born dumb. He raised his hands and eyes to heaven, glanced appealingly from one to the other of the little company, but never attempted to open his lips. And for the best possible reason : he had nothing in the world to say.

Mrs. de Robert paused for a moment to gather breath, then with choler undiminished, and voluble as before, she took the Doctor in hand. If his meek and contrite uncle deserved a birching, surely the unabashed and even jaunty nephew merited little less than the bastinado. There he sat showing a merry countenance, hands impocketed, just raising himself from time to time on his chair, all the while eying his terrible kinswoman with equanimity and defiance.

' 'Tis little enough I have to say to *you*,' began Mrs. de Robert. ' But 'twill be a pepperer, I warrant you. You are a young man— thirty-five or thereabouts, I take it. How comes it that you should be running about the world in this harum-scarum fashion, instead of staying at home and maintaining a wife and family? What could put it into your head, that were there a million to be disposed of you would get so much as a groat? Of what use would money be to such a good for nothing? as well throw it into the sea at once. I don't wonder, I am sure, that you found your way here in this slinking, underhand fashion. You know you had not so much as a word to say for yourself. But when you took me to be one of those weak creatures, imposed upon by soft speeches and artful flatteries, you were vastly mistaken. I saw through you from the first.'

'My dear madam,' began the Doctor, in the most cheerful tones, 'never had I a more agreeable task than that of vindicating myself in your eyes. But let me dispose of your aspersions one at a time. First of all, you find fault with me for being a bachelor, and you seem to think that no man can be worth his weight—well, say in hay, that being as cheap a commodity as any, unless he has a better-half and a round dozen of youngsters. But, permit me to observe, history proves the exact contrary. The men who have been worth their weight in gold, we find, were bachelors. There is that shining luminary, Newton ; that prince of philosophers, Locke, both unmarried men, to say nothing of other immortals as plentiful as blackberries. In fact, to have reached his prime and remained a bachelor is the most splendid eulogium that can be pronounced upon any man. He has sacrificed himself for humanity in general, and the good of ages to come. His portion

consists of crusts watered with tears and damp
stockings, instead of buttered bannocks and
slippers warmed for him by a loving spouse.
Well, now for your next indictment. I am
roaming about the world in vagabond fashion,
say you ; but consider a moment. I am no
fairy prince possessed of an invisible cloak.
Science has invented no method of compressing
one's ponderosity into a nutshell. I was obliged
to come as I am, bring my fourteen stone of
flesh, bone, and muscle, or stay at home.'

Mrs. de Robert was fain to interrupt this
tirade and begin her third castigation. The
Doctor would be heard to the end.

' Finally, you hurl invectives at me for not
having made myself known to you before.
The subterfuge was resorted to in order to
spare your feelings. Supposing you had con-
ceived a violent antipathy to me, how painful
to have to manifest it openly, and send me
empty-handed away! Such an incognito was
dictated by the most delicate scruples that can
actuate the human mind.'

' A fig for your scruples!' cried Mrs. de

Robert. ' You are a specious-tongued machi-
nator, that is what you are. However, there
is more excuse for you than for a minister of
religion. What can you say for yourself?'
she said, now turning waspishly to the third
delinquent. 'Much good have you learned
from Bible and Prayer-book, whatever you
may have taught the poor blackies. I am sure
I am as fit to go and convert the heathen
myself. How could a preacher of the Gospel
reconcile himself to such shifts and double-
dealing? What do you set us nodding about
on Sundays except righteous men and duty
to one's neighbours, and so forth ? But 'tis
always so. Those who pretend to be better
than others are the worst.'

She paused, not from want of arguments
but lack of breath, and the priest adroitly
seized the chance of getting in a word. It was
the thin end of the wedge. He knew well
enough, if difficult for him to stop Mrs. de
Robert, still more difficult would it be for her
to stop him. Invaluable result of his training!
What would not many of us give to attain

such perfect mastery of any situation that presents itself—such entire self-reliance under the most perplexing circumstances!

With ready insinuation and a smile, half-sarcastic, half-patronizing, he began :

' My fellow-culprits are well able to take care of themselves, or I could say much on their behalf, and every word thus uttered would have double force when applied to myself. If it is natural, even praiseworthy, to desire wealth for honourable self-advance-ment, the good of one's family, philanthropic objects, and the like, is not much more to be said for those craving wealth without any personal motive whatever——'

' Hear, hear!' cried the irrepressible Doctor, clapping his hands.

' Plausible as a parson, they may well say,' put in Mrs. de Robert, letting, however, the speaker go on.

' Had I journeyed hither from a remote corner of the globe in hope of mending my family fortunes, placing a son out in the world, providing a daughter with dowry, and obtaining comforts for my old age, where was the blame? But fill my pockets with gold, send me back whence I came a millionnaire, freight the ship that bears me with treasure of all kinds—not so much as the value of a loaf of bread should I regard as my own.'

'Hear, hear!' again cried the Doctor.

The elder Derrober listened with sympathetic interest. Prue looked deeply impressed. Sabina enjoyed the scene intensely now that the altercation had taken a milder form, and she dreaded no more storms. Miss Ivory, making signs to one and another of her guests, demurely passed them a supplementary cup of tea.

'That is always how you parsons talk. You are all saints in your own estimation. But as this fine talk costs us nothing, let us sit it out!' Mrs. de Robert exclaimed.

More impressively the speaker went on.

'Your money would raise schools and churches in the wilderness, ransom the slave, spread the love of the English name to remote corners of the globe, teach the savage to bend the knee to the only God.'

'Hear, hear!' a third time cried the Doctor.

'With aims like these, was I not justified in acting as I have done?' pursued the priest, 'in taking what seemed the most likely course to bring about my wishes? We have no magic arts wherewith to fascinate others and force them into doing our will. We can but use such weapons as we possess. It seemed natural to expect some antipathy, even prejudice, from you, towards one of my calling. I hoped, I believed, that having learned to know the man, you would no longer recoil from the Jesuit!'

'A Jesuit!' cried Mrs. de Robert aghast; then the recollection of the mysterious letters, ' S. J.,' came back to her, and she saw it all.

Never had wolf more cunningly disguised itself in sheep's clothing. Her wrath and indignation knew no bounds; but there was something in the priest's manner and appearance that compelled her to exercise self-

control. Her cup of ire was full to over-
flowing. She could not fling sarcasm and
invective at him as at the mute uncle and
aggressive nephew.

'Far be it from me to deny my calling,'
was the quiet reply. 'Can any show more
striking examples of flesh subdued to will;
the human Ego transformed into a passive in-
strument for good?'

'Humph!' cried Mrs. de Robert. 'There
are two sides to that question. However, go
on, sir.'

'I will strike out that word " good," then,
since it displeases you,' the priest added
gravely, 'and say, instead, "for what he believes
to be good"——'

'Hear, hear!' a fourth time ejaculated the
lively Doctor.

The speaker continued:

'Now, I take not the slightest credit to
myself for the fact, but it is incontestable. I
am no longer a certain individuality, like
other men, a bundle of personalities. I am a
mere agent, an automaton—a piece of machi-

nery in human form. We cannot help ourselves. We Jesuits must be single-minded,
whether we will or no. Do we not travel
from one end of the known globe to the other
with nothing in the shape of property but a
Bible? Even that does not entirely belong to
us. No matter the climate or the task, the
perils that beset us, the privations we have to
undergo, like soldiers we obey the word of
command. No murmurs ever escape our
lips.' ·

'Every word, so far, Gospel-truth,' inter-
rupted the Doctor.

The speaker continued, with milder insinuation than before:

'Whatever thoughts you may harbour in
your mind against my order, let us be reconciled on these terms. I come to you as a
mendicant on behalf of the Christ you believe
in, as well as myself. Whether I go away
empty-handed or no, I shall ever bear you
kindliest feeling, and this pilgrimage to the
home of my ancestors will be remembered as
one of the brightest episodes of my existence.

Madam and dear cousin, take my hand in token of reconcilement.'

The climax was so unexpected, the sudden turn given to affairs so irresistible, that a little electric shock seemed to run through the company. Even Mrs. de Robert felt the thrill, and looked dazed, dumbfounded. Never was painful position more adroitly changed, never stormy feeling allayed with quieter magic.

But when the speaker, not content with taking his kinswoman's reluctantly extended hand, respectfully stooped down and saluted her on each cheek with the kiss of peace, the general enthusiasm knew no bounds.

The elder Derrober started from his seat as if he had been straightway ordered to do so, and went up to Sabina and Prue, according the same fraternal salute.

The Doctor clapped his hands to see, looked wistfully at Miss Ivory, advanced a step towards her, then drew back.

Uncle and nephew obtained a hand-shake from Mrs. de Robert, not for the life of them venturing to ask for more.

Then followed a general hand-shaking and interchange of friendly little speeches. All was agreeable flutter and commotion.

Miss Ivory, meantime, turned to her old friend with the most sparkling grace imaginable, and as she glanced round with a charming smile, thus commented upon the day's event:

'One thing seems certain, you and I, Mrs. de Robert, hardly need to set forth, like Don Quixote and Sancho Panza, in search of romance and adventure. Romance and adventure have begun at home!'

CHAPTER III.

CLERICAL HIDE-AND-SEEK.

 NO less curious scene was taking place just beyond the precincts of the little glade.

By dint of womanly tact and diplomacy Miss Ivory had extracted a promise from both the Vicar and the Curate to join her woodland company. If only for a few minutes, they must come, she said, in order to show the sincerity of their reconciliation.

Now, such an invitation to both was precisely a case of powder and jam. They were to gulp down the nauseous dose of each other's presence as best they could for the sake of a word, a smile, from the beautiful Eugenia

As to reconciliation, there was every induce-
ment to shake hands and appear on friendly
terms. Their very existence—in other words,
her good opinion—depended on their bearing
to each other.

The Vicar, in most matters an exceedingly
self-controlled man, able to keep his impulses
and passions well in hand, found it none the
less difficult to be cool now.

Mr. Bacchus, mercurial, inflated with vanity
one moment, self-depreciatory to morbidness
the next, felt, as he afterwards expressed it,
on the edge of a precipice. He was determined to humble himself in the Vicar's presence, and not to quarrel, even if incensed
and exasperated beyond human endurance.
But if Miss Ivory's name were brought forward he could not be responsible for his
actions, he said. He could not, really.

Disagreeable as it was to the Vicar to have
to meet the Curate, and still more repugnant
as it was to Mr. Bacchus to encounter Mr.
Meridian, the pair found it impossible to resist
Eugenia's fascinations. If the chance pre-

sented itself of spending half an hour in her presence, they must seize on it, no matter how dearly purchased the pleasure. So it was now. The fire would scorch and inflict cruel smarts; the flame was magnetically attractive to these poor moths as to any flitting about our candle. Go to the sylvan meeting-place they must and would.

There was, however, just one comfortable straw to clutch at. They might miss each other, or all but miss each other—that is to say, the one might come just as his rival was departing, or the reverse. A fortuitous concatenation of events might entail upon them only a formal 'How-d'ye-do?' and 'Good-day.'

The step taken by the Rev. Mr. Bacchus to ensure a solution of the knotty point was highly characteristic. Having finished his sermon, he pulled out of his pocket a penny-piece, and tossed up for it—heads if the Vicar should quit Eugenia and her friends early, tails if he should arrive late. Heads won ; so the Curate, with great alacrity, decided to join the picnic-party towards the close of the afternoon.

Mr. Meridian's resolve was promptly made. 'That unconscionable Bacchus,' he said, 'is sure to tire everybody out by getting there too soon. I may just manage to miss him by going at the last moment.'

And then he said to himself, and pretended to believe it, that his only motive for going at all was the satisfaction of Miss Ivory. He wished to show her that he was as good as his word, and that the Curate, provided he behaved like a gentleman for the future, had nothing in the world to fear from him.

Thus, as ill-luck would have it, the two men timed their setting out so as to approach the meeting-place very nearly at the same moment.

Miss Ivory's choice of a rendezvous lent itself to the clerical hide-and-seek that now followed. Hopeful as they felt about escaping each other's society, both the Vicar and the Curate realized the necessity of caution. Anyhow, they would not for worlds encounter each other on the way.

The woodland meeting-place was the slope of a wooded hill commanding a view of More-cambe Bay. Above this lawny opening were the coppice-woods, a compact mass of greenery and shadow; and higher still the broad, breezy fell, divided by a road.

Now, so long as their roads remained in the open, there was no risk of a meeting. The Vicar started from one point, the apex of a V, the Curate from another: they could not possibly meet till they had nearly reached their journey's end. Briskly and confidently they made the best of their way to the edge of the wood; but when once they plunged in it was a different matter. The paths made by nut-gatherers and bilberry-pickers were few and far between. They must take the first downward one they could find, or none at all, and every step must necessarily lead them nearer to each other, each supposing the other to be on the way. To meet anyhow was disagreeable enough; to meet in a path only wide enough to admit of one was something more than disagreeable under the circumstances.

The Curate was the first to get into the wood, and no sooner there than his behaviour resembled that of a hare sniffing the harriers abroad. He stopped short, pricked up his ears, glanced hither and thither, although, of course, there was nothing to see but green boughs, went on a step farther, then looked and listened again. No; he could not so much as hear the rustling of a leaf. Nobody was about but himself. At the same time he discreetly left the path he had chosen and struck into a yet narrower one. Both led to the glade; the last, being beset with brambles, would hardly be chosen by a man so careful of his personal appearance as the Vicar. Next Mr. Meridian entered the wood. He took the first opening, and trudged on briskly. The afternoon was waning; scant time he should have with the little company at best. He must lose no time; not for worlds would he appear to regret the pledge accorded Eugenia;

nor was he less reluctant to seem negligent of her guests. He just glanced round, looked before and behind him to see if anybody was there, then hastened on.

As the pair thus playing hide-and-seek got nearer and nearer to the place of meeting, they must necessarily get nearer to each other, and reach the convergent point of the angle. But once within earshot of the little party drinking tea in the glade, they forgot their own concerns altogether.

The altercation had just begun. The first word that greeted their ears, uttered in a high key, and in a well-known voice, told them what had happened. The Vicar's little ruse had been detected. The storm of Mrs. de Robert's wrath was bursting in full fury over his partners in deceit.

Both stood still—Mr. Meridian listening as coolly as if he were a mere passer-by ; Mr. Bacchus relishing the scene with a schoolboy's love of imbroglio and mischief. The fault was not of his committing. He should get off scot-free this time. He could afford to laugh. Mr. Meridian's first impulse was disgust. It was a contretemps, a piece of checkmating. He had laid his plans differently, and he did not like to have them interfered with. In so far as Mrs. de Robert's anger concerned himself, he felt no anxiety. It was sufficiently disagreeable to be abused by a woman, certainly. You could not use the means of silencing her that you could naturally use in dealing with a man. But the ill taste, the vulgarity, would be hers, not his own. She might say what she pleased for aught he cared.

The pair continued to move on gingerly, just a step or two at a time, now halting altogether. Mrs. de Robert's tirades amused them mightily, and they liked to hear what the men had to say for themselves. They very soon became so absorbed as to be utterly oblivious of each other's probable presence. The slight rustling they now made was not even observed. With riveted attention they paused and listened. Now it was the Doctor speaking, his crisp, clear speech ringing through

the silence of the wood, every syllable being
caught with perfect distinctness. Next followed the vehement attack on the priest.
High-pitched almost to shrillness sounded
Mrs. de Robert's voice, more resembling
the cry of some discordant bird than mere
feminine utterance. In striking contrast came
the soft, silvery tones of her interlocutor.
Not a syllable of that well-turned apology
missed the ears of the pair, whilst emphatic
as the tapping of the woodpecker sounded
the ' Hear, hear' of the chorus.

The Vicar and the Curate now forgot that
little game of hide-and-seek just played so
cunningly.

When the priest left off speaking, and a
general silence intervened, both became so
anxious to see what was taking place that
they made a reckless plunge forward. The
path sloped towards a bit of copse bristling
with holly and bramble ; the copse was on a
deeper incline still, and ended in a broad dyke,
separating the wood from the open ground.
No sooner, therefore, was the hurried descent

begun than a halt became impossible. Were a horrid gulf or dangerous crevasse below, the pair, having once begun to go down, must keep on going down, and precipitate as had been the beginning, still more precipitate, according to the laws of motion, must be the end.

Without in the least suspecting what was about to happen, the Vicar and the Curate now tumbled, not only to the bottom of the ditch, but into each other's arms, greatly to their own discomfiture and the consternation of the little company there to see.

CHAPTER IV.

FRIENDS, LOVERS, AND RIVALS.

THE occurrence created a happy diversion.

'Deary me !' cried Mrs. de Robert, forgetting what she was afterwards pleased to call that Judas kiss.

> ' "Jack and Jill went up the hill,
> To fetch a pail of water ;
> Jack fell down and broke his crown,
> And Jill came tumbling after." '

Sabina and Prue recovered from the pleasing little shock of Mr. Derrober's salutation. The uncle and the priest looked on interested, but lazy. Miss Ivory and the Doctor ran forward to the aid of the unlucky adventurers.

Fortunately the dyke was dry, but it was deep and choked with brambles, nettles, and brushwood. Heated, discomposed, with rumpled garments, the pair once at the bottom found it no easy matter to regain their feet. Mr. Meridian, being the slighter of the two, was the first to emerge.

'Facilis est descensus Averni,' cried the Doctor, as he lent him a helping hand, 'and ofttimes thorny, sir, the path of pleasure as of virtue. However, here you are, and not much the worse, I hope, for your tumble.'

Mr. Meridian thanked him, shook the dust and thistle-down from his coat, adjusted his hat, and was himself in a moment, ready to dismiss the catastrophe from his mind altogether. It was a trifle not worth thinking about, he said.

The extrication of the Curate was a less easy matter. There he lay, his long limbs sprawling amid the brambles, the very picture of helplessness and dismay. Miss Ivory, however, with her parasol did good service, and at length he clambered up the steep sides of the ditch. He was not, however, inclined to drop the matter so quickly. Was it not an adventure ? and he adored adventures. Had he not evoked sympathy ? and he adored sympathy.

'What an extraordinary fact it is,' he said, 'one never knows where one is going ! We set out for a certain place, and the chances are ten to one that we arrive at exactly the opposite of that place. Who could have supposed, for instance, that there would be any risk to life or limb in crossing that little wood ? The wonder is we have come alive out of such a pitfall.'

The Vicar had nodded to the Curate ; the Curate had returned the greeting in the same easy fashion. Thus Mr. Bacchus's mind was set at rest upon one point. Mr. Meridian intended to let bygones be bygones, and be civil to him. His spirits rose.

'The least you could have done under the circumstances was to break a leg. Think of the romance of the situation,' Miss Ivory said. 'The Doctor's skill called into sudden requisi-

tion. All of us in a fever of anxiety. Yourself the hero of the hour.'

' Ah, a hero ! I should like for once in my
life to be that. The hero of a broken leg
would perhaps be better than nothing. But
no, some gloomy prognostic tells me I shall
never be even so much. I feel that I am
doomed to perpetual obscurity.'

' Renown is the easiest thing in the world,'
put in the Doctor. ' Contrive an ingenious
murder, and the whole world is talking about
you. There is the disagreeable feeling about
the thing, certainly, but you can be as sorry
as you please afterwards, and that makes all
right.'

The Curate seeing himself obliged to pay
his respects to Mrs. de Robert, Miss Ivory
took up the challenge.

' I hope you do not carry these abominable
theories into practice,' she said. This stranger
amused her. He was not handsome, nor
highly finished after the manner of Mr. Meridian. He evidently paid little attention to
his personal appearance, and was natural even

to bluntness. But he was very entertaining.

'A villain I am, must be of necessity,' he said. 'You don't suppose, do you, that a race is kept alive for six hundred years unless it consists of the deepest dyed scoundrels that ever throve on rapine, pillage, and murder? The saints, the wise folks, the meek, have all gone to the wall since history began, and coats-of-arms, family mottoes, and pedigrees just testify to the fact that our especial ancestors were about as bad as they could be, nothing more.'

'Would that I were a Montmorency for all that!' sighed Miss Ivory.

'Would that I could swear my great-grandfather was a grasshopper,' was the reply. 'To come into the world unencumbered of ancestral curses and crimes, as Father Adam himself. Ah! that is the kind of pedigree I would pay fifty pounds for at the Herald's Office. However, I have no reason to grumble with a genealogical tree that has brought me great expectations.'

'To be realised, I hope!' Eugenia said heartily.

'Wish not rashly! What is the thing we wish for when we get it ?—mere cobweb, thistle-down, soap-bubble ; but the condition of expectancy, that is true happiness. So do not suffer our kinswoman yonder to dismiss us summarily. I assure you, I wish for nothing better than to stay here and never go away at all—live at Hopedale to the close of my mortal career, perpetually waiting for something to my advantage!'

'And the longer Mrs. de Robert waits, the more claimants would, of course, be found,' she said. 'The De Robert family was given to wandering. One settled in Crim Tartary, and maybe married a Circassian ; a second went out with an explorer to the South Seas, was made prisoner by the natives, married a maiden and turned savage ; a third disguised himself as a Mussulman for the sake of seeing Timbuctoo, and for aught we know his descendants may be that to this day. Now, if Mrs. de Robert could only advertise

for her husband's next of kin in the newspapers, not only of Europe, but of the entire
globe, what a motley invasion we should have!'

'Where meantime would be the spoil?'
the Doctor said, with a little grimace. 'This
polyglot proceeding, I trow, would soon swallow it up as neatly as a boa-constrictor gulped
down an ox. How sorry, however, I am I
did not know of your romantic disposition
before! Instead of coming as plain Frank
Derrober, I would have disguised myself as
a Red Indian or some other equally engaging
survival. These romantic instincts, however,
I heartily approve of. To me it is a matter
of perpetual astoundment that the human
race does not come to a sudden standstill
—that women, be they the most prosaic who
ever kneaded a dumpling, can submit to be
courted by creatures wearing frock-coats and
chimney-pot hats.'

'Perhaps all is for the best,' the young lady
replied. 'If fine clothes were in vogue with
men also, would not the last line of demar-
cation between the two sexes disappear alto-

gether ? It seems to me that nothing but
the bonnet and the train distinguish the one
from the other.'

'It is handy certainly to have such dis-
tinctions in the case of professional folk,' the
Doctor replied. 'Suppose I had a wife, and
that wife an M.D., but for the bonnet what
imbroglios would arise! She blunders in cutting off a leg, I am had up for incompetence.
I poison a patient by misadventure, the poor
woman hangs for it. Lawyers and advocates
too. A nice time they would have of it
united in holy matrimony but for the bonnet.
The judge's gown conferred upon Mrs. Brief
by mistake. Mr. Brief laid violent hands on
by doctor and nurse when his better half
is taken ill. The legal fireside would be a
Pandemonium, Blackstone a bone of conten-
tion, but for the bonnet.'

Do women marry men for their wit ? Such
was the question uppermost in the Vicar's
mind that afternoon as he watched Eugenia
and her companion. For the first time he
began to regard these next of kin in the light

of possible rivals. The epigrammatic Doctor disconcerted, even alarmed him. He saw that these scintillations and flashes of wit and esprit, this apt, ready, telling speech, impressed and entertained Miss Ivory—that she was laid under a charm. Dr. Derrober, so at least thought the Vicar, had not much else to recommend him. He was confessedly a poor man. He openly avowed that he had little to boast of in the way of worldly position. He was furthermore a man wedded to ideas, a speculator, a theorist, an intellectual vagabond, here to-day, there to-morrow, the last in the world likely to win honours of place or rise in the social scale.

Nor could he be called personally attractive, Mr. Meridian thought; he seemed an excellent fellow in the main—frank, pleasant, far from being common, much less contemptible—that was all to be said in his favour. Except for his really remarkable gift of speech, there was nothing to distinguish him from the crowd.

Seeing, however, that he did possess this

faculty of saying clever things, and that Miss
Ivory listened to him with alacrity, the Vicar
did not like the look of it. He determined by
hook or by crook, by fair means or foul, to
settle the matter of Mrs. de Robert's next of
kin as summarily as possible. The charmer
must be forthwith got rid of. Meantime, the
worse luck for him, he had delegated the task
of entertaining the strangers to Eugenia.
Never had over-confidence led him into a
graver blunder. From her kindly feeling for
the Curate, irritating as it was, he knew that
he had little or nothing to fear. But women
were so romantic, so given to enthusiasm!
Once their imaginations are touched, there is
no accounting for them. Yes, the sooner the
pair of Transatlantic travellers were sent home
the better.

It might seem inconsistent in Mr. Meridian
to dwell upon these matters so seriously now.
After what had passed between himself and
Miss Ivory a few days before, surely most
men would have given up the case as hopeless. Like the haughty lover in the song,

they would have turned from the lady with
the farewell :

> ‘ If she be not fair to me,
> What care I how fair she be ?’

Not of this complexion the Vicar of Hopedale. He was a man of the world, widely
experienced in affairs, and possessed a keen
insight into the human heart. He knew how
often mere impulse and inclination are worsted
by force of circumstances ; how complex are
the springs of action ; how ofttimes motiveless
and involuntary appears the conduct of life in
gravest crises. That Eugenia did not love
him, and would not hearken to his suit now,
was no sort of argument that she would never
marry him. At least, so he reasoned, as he
discontentedly watched her in animated conversation with the Doctor; whilst to his share
fell a far less agreeable tête-à-tête with Mrs.
de Robert.

‘ You are uncommonly nimble in getting
out of a ditch,’ were her first words, accompanied by a̗ mischievous chuckle.

He coolly brushed some thistle-down still

sticking to his garments ; then added, as he took a seat beside her :

'And as nimble, you must confess, in getting out of a difficulty. You cannot deny that I hit upon a capital expedient for introducing you to those obnoxious next of kin.'

'A nice sort of a person you are for a clergyman,' Mrs. de Robert said, no longer wrathful, but nettled at having been taken in. 'Up till now I should have believed anything in the world you chose to tell me. Yes, had you said my tabby cat was coal-black or milk-white, I should have said : "If Mr. Meridian calls her black or white, black or white she must be, though all the world call her a tabby."'

'I am delighted to hear you say so,' the Vicar replied, following Eugenia and her cavalier with furtive glances.

'Delighted to be told to your face that henceforth I shall never believe a word you say!' cried Mrs. de Robert.

'Believe in what I do, and I shall be perfectly satisfied,' retorted the Vicar. 'You are,

I am sure, at heart charmed to find that these delightful personages are really your relations. You were praising them to the skies but yesterday.'

'You won't hear me praise them to the skies any more,' was the indignant reply. 'Praise people who find pleasure in hoaxing an old woman like me?—not I!'

'Nay, the jest was innocent enough, and perfectly justifiable,' the Vicar answered in the same quietly satiric tones. 'If all is fair in love and war, all is certainly fair in a game of scramble like this.'

He turned to his old friend with a penetrating look, and added in a low voice only audible to herself:

'You seem to forget that these good people want money.'

'Then,' she said in a pet, 'give 'em the money—give 'em everything there is—and send 'em about their business!'

CHAPTER V.

A WOODLAND CONFERENCE.

HAT will not spirit, wit, under-standing do for a man ?
Here was this stranger charm-ing Miss Ivory, the fastidious Miss Ivory ; by virtue of speech only, turning a common hour and an every-day scene into romance and adventure, riveting her attention as if some delightful drama were being enacted before her eyes.

After the climax and anticlimax that had just occurred, the little party broke up into twos and threes. Mr. Bacchus helped Prue and Sabina to fill their baskets with wild strawberries for the children. Mr. Derrober

23—2

and Father de Robert paced the glades, deep
in theological discussion. Only Mrs. de
Robert and the Vicar remained seated, con-
fabulating amicably as a pair of lovers after a
somewhat hot debate. There was this to be
said for Mr. Meridian, as she admitted afterwards—he could always talk people over.
Were he to encounter his Satanic Majesty
himself, and be entrapped into an argument,
he would succeed in talking him over.

There was no reason therefore why Eugenia
and the Doctor should not quit the others
now. The little wood just above the glade
led to a fine bit of breezy heath, and when
once you began to ramble over it, you felt
inclined to go on rambling, especially in good
company.

The young lady had taken off her hat, and
a charming apparition she made, with which
to startle the rabbits and multitudinous little
birds piping in the bushes.

Her tall, erect figure never looked to better
advantage than in a light summer dress such
as she wore now—hers, too, the face to be

seen to best advantage out of doors. No more need had the wild rose to shun inspection in the clear light of day, and the one as free from blemish as the other.

The very last thing uppermost in Eugenia's mind, however, was her own appearance just then ; nor did she pay the slightest attention to her companion's. He interested her. Could a paragon of his sex do more? She wanted to hear of his history—his past experiences—above all, of himself. The first sympathetic chord touched, the keynote struck of a harmony capable of infinite variation, intercourse becomes progressive and easy.

' You must wonder—you are bound to wonder,' he began, ' how it comes about that two men, presumably neither dolts nor knaves, should be failures. What good can there be in fellows who have not sense and self-preservation enough to make somebodies of themselves—in other words, to get on in the world ? We are not successes, my uncle and I ; were it otherwise, we should hardly be here

—a couple of millionnaires would not be at the trouble of crossing the Atlantic on the strength of an advertisement.'

He stopped; and, very carefully extricating Eugenia's dress from a bramble, went on:

'Having come, we ought at least to tell you who and what we are. To begin with my uncle, he is a nineteenth-century saint for you, if any breathes! Cross America by one Pacific railway, re-cross it by the other, and you won't find his match. But a dead failure from his cradle; and wherefore? Because he unluckily came into the world hampered with a conscience. He is a preacher by trade—did you guess it?—and, as a preacher, would have fattened and thriven, but for that terrible business of a conscience. He began—was ever such a piece of insanity? —by preaching against slavery before the War of Secession was thought of; and, of course, that wouldn't do. They clapped him into prison; but no sooner was he out again than he began preaching against fratricidal wars, and, of course, was locked up again for that.

Then, when things were settled a bit, he must needs take up the subject of political corruption. Could madness go farther? I assure you, although he would never open his lips on these matters, he has been almost as much of a martyr as John Brown or Uncle Tom in the lady's novel. He has just escaped St. Lawrence's gridiron, and that is all.'

Meanwhile, one thought was uppermost in Eugenia's generous mind; one question was on her lips she hesitated to utter. Did poverty form part of this evil fortune? Would the money Mrs. de Robert had to give prove a real blessing to these two wanderers?

'Is there a God of Smugness in the Roman calendar?' continued the Doctor. 'Was ever any day dedicated to smooth-tongued slipperiness and unctuous compliance? If so, these be my gods; on their altars shall my incense smoke. Henceforth, I will be warned by my uncle's example, and sleek Prosperity shall be my only fetish. Now, I ought to have succeeded—got on in the world, as the phrase goes—if ever any man did, especially in the medical profession. Never so benignant, so cheery a doctor! Half the folks who came to consult me I sent away, for the excellent reason that they ailed nothing. Why should people ever ail anything if they exercised as much self-preservation as a hermit - crab? The other half I rated soundly for their impudence in coming to me at all. What business had they with their coughs, carbuncles, disordered livers, dyspepsia, and the like? None whatever. Illness is just so much wickedness; disease but another name for vice. If we are not punished for our own sins, 'tis for those of our forefathers, which is much the same thing. I gave it 'em soundly, depend on it.'

'You would hardly get rich on such a practice as that,' Eugenia said, smiling.

'I ought to have gilded my horse's oats like Caligula, and sandwiched my bread with bank-notes like blockade-runners in the last war. But who was ever paid for speaking the truth? My professional earnings of a twelve-

mouth came to how much, think you? Just
enough money to cover the expense of pens,
ink, and paper used in prescriptions. Ah!
those prescriptions! I should like you to
have seen some of them! Drugs and nostrums
were left out altogether. The treatment I
applied was of another kind, and far less
acceptable. Well, I soon gave up physic as a
losing concern, and took to what is called a
professorial chair. That was hardly the thing
to answer in my case, either. My pathology,
you see, was so eccentric; my pharmacopœia
so revolutionary. Before I had thundered
forth anathemas on medical science as now
practised for the space of three months, I was
politely asked to resign. That check did not
abate my ardour. I said to myself there
were more ways than one of putting a truth
before the world. First catch your hare, as
the cookery-book says, and then proceed to
prepare it for table. We now set up a kind
of partnership, my uncle and myself, and our
first co-venture was a newspaper. I took in
hand the facts, my senior the morality depart-

ment; the business part of the concern was left pretty much to look after itself. Of course,. our newspaper was not to be like other newspapers. News—in other words, the vulgarities, trivialities, and common-places chronicled elsewhere—we left out altogether. We wanted not to tell people what their neighbours were doing, but what they might be doing themselves ; not what was going on in the way of politics, theology, philanthropy, and the like, but what ought to be going on. In fact, our journal was a journal of Might-be's—of notable Perhapses.'

Miss Ivory could not resist a laugh.

' Did the paper pay ?' she asked.

' Its success was brilliant—for exactly two weeks. For three weeks it was tolerated. At the end of that time no one would take a copy, even gratis. Nothing so much of a drug in the market as an idea. Of course you have found that out long ago.'

' And what was your next idea ?' she asked.

' Does all this really interest you ?' he said,

looking at her suddenly with a penetrative glance. He was evidently struck by her attitude. She seemed to relish the narrative keenly ; but was it so indeed ? Could it be ? Could the experiences of two shabby, way-worn strangers really absorb this beautiful, high-spirited, much-admired girl ?

Her direct, artless answer reassured him.

' Why should I pretend to be interested ?' she replied, quite naturally. ' Pray go on.'

Evidently much gratified, the relator continued :

' Of late years, the rest of the Might-be's have been joint concerns, my uncle furnishing the soul, myself the sinews of the affair ; in other words, I undertook the practical details, he devoting himself to the theoretical. We were of one mind. We wanted something in the way of existence less cut and dry, less hackneyed, less threadbare, than that with which most people seem satisfied. Our beginnings in this line were glorious. Had you been in America at the time, you would have heard our names noised abroad, I warrant you.

Our model society was pronounced to be a foreshadowing of the millennium itself. We began by ferreting out a few idealists like ourselves, women as well as men, and very charming companions they were. All would have gone smoothly to this day but for one trifling drawback. Sanctify labour by all means. Cultivate the principle of social equality at any cost. Deprave no fellow-creature into a professional turnspit or japanner. But what if ye have not so much as a lean hen to pop into the pot? What if the shoes of the community wear out, and there is no money wherewith to buy leather? This soon came to be our predicament. We found that, like the greedy old gods of old, ideas had gobbled up their own children. These co-workers with us in the good cause were all rich in faith and hope only, poor in material wealth as the Greek cynic whom Charon bullied in vain for his fee of a penny. I think I have now given you a very fair notion of ourselves and our adventures. Whatever we may not be, we are honest.'

There was a touch of wistfulness, rather than regret, in his voice, as he uttered the closing sentence, and once more he looked earnestly at his fair listener.

They now found themselves on the breezy ridge above the wood. A gate invites a halt, and finding one here, they rested against it before going back.

How sweet and peaceful the scene on which they gazed! They had their faces turned from the bay, and looked on the sweet inland landscape, broken heath in the foreground, delicately empurpled as a plum ere yet its bloom is swept off; beyond, meadows dotted with kine, orchards and gardens from which peeped many a house-top. The venerable church-tower was also visible. A warm rosy glow filled the heavens. Sweet scents of honeysuckle and wild clematis reached them where they stood.

'I will say so much for ourselves,' added the speaker. 'We have never been envious; never wasted a regret upon the snug existence of other folks. As to my uncle, he doesn't

know what self means. He is the most dis-
interested mortal that ever breathed ; whilst,
for my own part, I have been a vagabond by
inclination, a ne'er-do-weel, a happy-go-lucky,
of my own free will—till now.'

He stopped short, and a strange expression
came into his face. The careless vivacity, the
easy self-assertion vanished ; instead might be
read deep feeling and passionate introspec-
tion.

' My uncle has no need to regret that his
life must be pronounced a failure. He has
loved all women, and been beloved in blame-
less, sisterly fashion by not a few. Millions—
the most dazzling position—the applause of
the world — would hardly have made him
happier. My own case is wholly different. I
have hitherto laughed sentiment to scorn. I am
now justly punished. I have seen the woman
who makes me forswear my former creeds.
It is all of a piece,' he added, after a moment's
pause. ' Wherever I go, whatever fortunes
overtake me, I shall have the Lady of Hopedale, and the scenes through which she moves,

before my eyes. The picture is perfect. None I have hitherto beheld are to be compared to it. None I shall ever gaze on in the far distant future will banish it from my memory.'

Miss Ivory tried to smile away his seriousness, but he insisted on being heard to the end, and went on in the same tones :

'This something to my advantage, forsooth! Let it go! What more do I want? What else can heaven give me? I came here poor in many senses—above all, beggared in one. Few men, I suppose, reach middle life without succumbing to a beautiful impression —being wholly mastered by deep feeling. Such, however, has been my own case. I now go away rich, then, for I have at last learned what it is to adore !'

'Had we not better go back?' said Miss Ivory, as soon as she had recovered self-possession enough to say anything.

He assented silently, and, as one in a dream, retraced his steps by her side. The

entire man seemed transformed by the mood
that had taken possession of him.   No more
jests ; no more sharp sayings ; not a single
epigram dropped from his lips that evening.

CHAPTER VI.

THE WOODEN HORSE.

 FEW days later the good folks of
Hopedale were in a state of the
greatest possible commotion.

It had already been noised abroad that
something was to happen ; in other words,
that the denouement of the little De Robert
drama was at hand. Divers rumours floated
in the air. A speedy transfer of the family
treasure would shortly take place under
strictest police supervision. The division of
the spoil would follow close upon the heels of
this event, and what then ? Did Mrs. de
Robert and her beautiful companion really
intend, then, to quit Hopedale for once and for

all? The Wooden Horse, as it slowly rumbled
through the streets of Troy, excited hardly
more interest than the vehicle containing these
much-talked-of heirlooms.   As the cumber-
some conveyance, in aspect not unlike a
prison van, moved slowly up the village street,
guarded by Mr. Rapp, the local constable, all
windows were thrown wide, all faces were
agape.

   The phenomenon, too, as in the case of the
Wooden Horse, announced without doubt the
close of a long drawn out series of events, the
final disposal of Mrs. de Robert's next of
kin, and the something they were to hear of
to their advantage.   Speculation was first
busy as to the contents of that well-guarded
van.   Everybody had heard vaguely of the
works of art, the chased silver, the jewellery,
to be distributed among the lucky claimants ;
but, excepting Mr. Meridian, no outsider had
as yet been favoured with so much as a glimpse
of the treasures.   It was, however, reported
abroad that before their ultimate dispersion
these rarities, owing to an obliging suggestion

of the Vicar, were really to be exposed to view.
In other words, the drawing-room at Hopedale was to be turned into a species of local
museum for the space of two days. Mr.
Meridian, quite naturally, did not wish his
parishioners to be deprived of such an opportunity of improving their minds : pictures by
Murillo, Rubens and Teniers were not to be
seen every day.

Besides the heirlooms proper, such as the
armour worn by heroic De Roberts at Poitiers
and Bosworth Field, the chased silver plate
more than once pledged for St. George and
Merry England, the jewels worn by fair ances-
tresses at Court, there was a valuable collection of miscellaneous antiquities, amassed by
the late Mr. de Robert himself. It enchanted
the village folks to learn that these treasures
were to be exhibited for the public good, and
that before their final dispersion everybody
was to be gratified with a sight of them.
Everybody, moreover, was to be invited to a
soirée at the Manor House, given in honour of
these events.

24—2

The Wooden Horse—in other words, the covered van piled to the roof—suggested all kinds of pleasurable excitement. Next in interest after the Wooden Horse came the fate of the warriors. What would be the final issue of this miniature siege of Troy? Was it to be a case of share and share alike, or would one more fortunate than the rest obtain the lion's share? What with one question and another, tiptoe curiosity and liveliest interest were the order of the day at Hopedale. No one had the remotest idea what would be the end of the affair; but end it must somehow, and that soon.

Summer was on the wane, autumn was at hand, and the claimants one and all began to talk of departure. The priest might be said already to have taken his departure from Hopedale. He was paying short visits here and there in that part of the country, appearing at the Vicarage from time to time, and in apostolic phrase charging Mr. Meridian at a convenient time to call for him. Meantime, who so busy as Mrs. de Robert's faithful henchman ? Touchy as she had ever been regarding these next of kin, she bristled up like a porcupine whenever their names were so much as mentioned now.

'Do as you please with the rubbish,' she said, in allusion to the contents of the Wooden Horse. 'Give it to knaves, fools or idiots— throw it into the sea for aught I care ; only don't let me hear another word about the business.'

Mr. Meridian and Eugenia therefore took secret counsel together, and, in spite of some drawbacks, well were these tête-à-tête interviews relished by the Vicar. Lovers, at least of his stamp, never lose patience ; and seeing at last that Lewti was kind, he felt momentarily hopeful. Her kindness might only indicate contrition, perhaps mere pity ; it heartened him for all that. The real sting of these confidential talks was that they were destined so soon to end.

Mrs. de Robert and Eugenia seemed determined to quit Hopedale, at least for a time, and when she was once beyond reach, where

would be his prospect of success then? The
more expeditious, too, his settlement of the
property, the sooner they would go away.
Yet so long as the matter were allowed to
drag on, he was but keeping a rival in the
field. A rival, no doubt, this American
stranger was, perhaps with fewer chances of
winning the prize than himself; but a rival in
the field for all that. Vain the effort to shut
his eyes to the fact. The epigrammatic doctor
was over head and ears in love with Miss
Ivory. She would surely never dream of
marrying him; but what if he prevented her
from marrying another? Eugenia's friendliness to the Curate was sufficiently irritating.
Her growing interest in this stranger seemed
little less than maddening.

Yes, the Derrobers must be got rid of at
any price.

This business was to the Vicar of Hopedale
as a fit of sickness to some unhappy convict.
Convalescence in such a case means solitude,
hard fare, monotonous toil; aches and pains,
on the contrary, go with comparative ease,

gentle treatment, recreation. One moment recovery is ardently longed for, the next it is as sincerely prayed against. Thus was it with Mr. Meridian. Now he wanted this precious business to drag on indefinitely, now he wanted to get rid of it for once and for all. The pangs of jealousy and the dreary void suggested by Miss Ivory's departure alternately kicked the beam.

Eugenia could not help being kind to him now. He was hardly what is called an amiable man, but he had showed great willingness to sacrifice himself for her sake : in the first place, consenting to swallow the Curate's affront ; in the second, doing everything in his power to further her wishes, to facilitate her departure. It was really much more than good-natured, much more than considerate, and Eugenia felt really grateful. At the same time the sense of indebtedness tormented and oppressed her.

'So far all is settled then,' he said one afternoon, at the close of a longer confabulation than usual. 'Keep Mrs. de Robert to her word, and a fortnight hence there will be nothing to prevent you from going to Bongo.'

The words so jestingly uttered nevertheless betrayed an undercurrent of deep bitterness. She began to feel ashamed of those harmless dreams, and to ask herself if she ought not to give them up in order to please others—that is to say, Mr. Meridian.

With heightened colour and some temper, she replied:

' Have not all of us a Bongo? Everybody at some time or other, I am sure, must wish to glance beyond one's own cabbage-beds. Why should I be blamed for longing like a child to go to the fair?'

' Nay, did I ever blame you?' he said in a quiet voice. ' You misunderstand me—that is all.'

Those proud cold words made matters worse still. To Miss Ivory's impatient mood succeeded a quick, generous revulsion of feeling.

' You are very kind,' she answered, still with heightened colour.

'Oh, for Heaven's sake, do not thank me!' was all he said.

The little speech, no sooner spoken, was repented of, and to this outburst of feeling succeeded icy reserve and matter-of-fact friendliness.

No one could be more impersonal than Mr. Meridian when he chose, no one more disliked the notion of unveiling his inner self to others. But, constantly as he was thrown with Eugenia now, reticence became impossible. The figure of the stranger, ever hovering in the background, could not be got rid of any more than that of the Curate.

In the eyes of the world, his parishioners, his friends, and his household, he was not in the least changed. He went through the routine of daily duty with the same precision. He shirked no disagreeable or agitating encounter. To outsiders he was affable, courtly, and obliging as before. But all the while a tremendous struggle was taking place within. He was wrestling with himself as men seldom wrestle but once in a lifetime.

CHAPTER VII.

VISIONS OF HAROUN EL RASCHID.

ABINA and Prue sat busily darning stockings when their host burst in with the wonderful tidings. He had just come from Hopedale, and in the village street had encountered the vanload on its way to the Manor—in other words, the Wooden Horse.

'Have you heard of it?' he cried, throwing off his hat and tumbling into an armchair, heated and breathless. 'Thousands, tens of thousands, hundreds of thousands of pounds' worth of treasure awaiting distribution among you all at Hopedale this very moment.'

Sabina dropped her sock and took off her

spectacles, Prue laid down her stocking, and both looked up with delight and bewilderment.

They were so happy under this friendly roof, so thoroughly at home with the Curate and his children, so much in love with this verdant dale nestled beside the northern sea, that they hardly wanted anything more to happen at all.

The. much-speculated-upon, much-longed-for something to their advantage seemed already a reality. Had they not both found what they wanted—romance, new experiences, new interests? Whilst to Prue the sojourn at Briardale had been richer in impressions still. She loved the Curate, but so long as they remained under the same roof it was a love that made her happy.

'Fetch me a glass of water, Georgie,' said Mr. Bacchus, still gasping with the heat. He always contrived to make his parochial rounds and transact other business in the hottest part of the day, and under the least comfortable conditions.

Georgie was, however, amusing baby, so Prue fetched, not ice-cold water, but a glass of home-made lemonade.

'Oh. dear!' cried the grateful Mr. Bacchus; 'how nice it is to be waited on and to get always twice as much as you ask for. That is my case since you ladies came, I am sure. And there you are, both at it again! Mending the children's socks, which I used to have to sit up at night to do before. It was something to my advantage when I got out of bed and let you in that night, and no mistake! Well, now to tell you the grand news. A vanload of treasure has just been conveyed to Hopedale under an escort of mounted police, and the distribution is really to take place in a week's time. I wish I stood in your shoes. The sweepings of that van would just set me up for life!'

'Oh! mayn't we just sweep it out with our new broom, papa?' asked Georgie, his youthful imagination fired by this highly-coloured account.

'We may do whatever we like, provided we

don't object to being belaboured black and
blue by the police afterwards,' was the satisfactory reply. 'Who could get all these
things together is a question that passes my
comprehension. Having got them, how anyone could keep them is a matter that would
puzzle Solomon and the Seven Sages of anti-
quity. Any addlepate can make a little
money. I dare say I could myself if I set to
work about it. But to keep a crown-piece
when once lodged in your pocket! That re-
quires the quintessence of wisdom. To go on
—diamonds big as hailstones——'

'Gold plate enough to furnish the Lord
Mayor's table. Silver that would coin into
thousands and tens of thousands of shil-
lings——'

'And not one odd threepenny-piece for poor
me?' asked Georgie.

'Don't interrupt,' Mr. Bacchus said. 'Let
me tell these ladies how rich they are going to
be. Now for the armour——'

The bare mention acted like a galvanic
battery upon Georgie. Forgetting all about

baby on his lap, he sat bolt upright,
staring at his father as if the glorious pageant
of Punch and Judy were being enacted before
his eyes.

Baby, meantime, not relishing such neglect,
set up a yell. Order had to be restored
before the Curate could proceed with his
narrative.

'I can get over the jewels and the plate,'
he went on. 'Diamonds are dug out of mines
every day, and anybody who has scraped
up money enough can eat off silver. But if I
live to be as old as the patriarchs, I shall
never understand how people can keep family
armour—coats of mail worn by their ancestors at the Siege of Troy, and other great
battles downwards. With museums being
opened, too, in the remotest regions of the
earth, one suit alone, if advantageously disposed of, would make one's fortune.'

'Might you not fit one on, papa?' asked
the fascinated Georgie. 'I should like to see
you and Mr. Meridian armed cap-à-pie with
visors drawn, and javelins a yard long, rushing

at each other, like the knights in Mrs. Mark-
ham's " History of England "!'

Mr. Bacchus looked as if he should like it
uncommonly, too, but once more bidding
Georgie not to interrupt, continued :

' Then the pictures ! The Murillo itself must
be worth the whole village of Briardale put
together; and the Titians, the Veroneses, the
Last Suppers, St. Peter Martyrs, and Madonna
de San Sistos, I confess myself fairly beaten.
I give it up, ladies ; you must set to work
and imagine how rich you are going to be.
I protest I cannot do it for you.'

Sabina and Prue were contented to discern
a vestige of reality behind the glimmering
haze of the Curate's description. They knew
that he had spoken metaphorically, but that
the metaphors meant something; and as the
Vicar of Wakefield said, anything, even a
gross of green spectacles in shagrin cases,
was better than nothing at all. They were
alike prepared for the best or the worst.
Anyhow, no one could rob them of this
idyllic life at Briardale.

'And when you get your great fortune, what are you going to do with it?'

This question was put by the Curate to Prue later on. The children were out with Jane. Sabina was in her room busily at work upon her diary.

'Bina,' had said the ever-sapient Edwin, in that immortal courtship, 'remember the wise dictum of the ancients, "Nulla dies sine linea" —No day without its line. Whatever happens or does not happen, put it down. A succinct record of the day's proceedings and probabilities affords the sure index of a methodical mind.'

The indefatigable little woman, partly on Edwin's account, and partly on her own, rigidly adhered to this precept, and her book was a bulky affair. She put down everything, whether it happened or whether it didn't, and a diary is apt to take gigantic proportions under such circumstances.

Prue and the Curate were alone when he asked the suggestive question:

'When you get your great fortune, what are you going to do with it?'

Prue always felt a feminine fluttering of the heart when she found herself alone with Mr. Bacchus. He was quite brother-like; he had never shown the slightest disposition to sentimentalize, he treating her just as he treated Sabina; yet to Prue the Curate's presence savoured of perpetual romance. His gaiety, his bonhommie, even his boyishness, were very engaging to her. She would not have seen him otherwise for the world.

Thus interrogated, she dropped her needlework, and looked up with a blush and a smile. In spite of silvery hairs mingled with the brown, and lines of care, Prue had by no means lost all outward charms. She was one of those women who really never grow old, and who, in a certain feminine sense, feel ever girlish and dreamy.

'What shall we do?' she said, with a touch of regret in her voice. 'Go home, I suppose, and never see Briardale any more.'

'I wish you would stay here,' the Curate said bluntly. 'Not if you really become rich as Jews, of course. My humble quarters would

not suit your ladyships then. You might carry
me away with you as your private chaplain
instead! But supposing you come off with
only a slice of the pudding—just a taste of the
goodies—why should you not stay? I would
take a better house. We would go in for a
sort of partnership. I am sure we should all
live together as happily as the people in
Noah's ark.'

'I am sure we should,' poor Prue said.

'Two people can live cheaper than one, and
three cheaper than two,' Mr. Bacchus went on.
'If you both consent, I will see about another
house at once. I assure you the thought of
spending the winter here alone drives me to
distraction.'

'It must be lonely for you,' Prue put in,
with a strange sinking of the heart. She
began to foresee what was coming.

'It is more than lonely, it is maddening,
and, I assure you, full of peril,' Mr. Bacchus
went on, growing gloomy and desperate. 'If
I am left alone in this wilderness of temptation I cannot answer for myself. You must

expect to hear the very worst of me. That is the pass things have come to.'

Sabina and Prue had only heard vaguely of the encounter between the rivals, but both could see how it stood with the Vicar and the Curate concerning the beautiful Miss Ivory.

'If you go away you may any morning, when glancing at the newspaper, find me sentenced to penal servitude for life, or something worse,' the Curate continued. 'We have patched up our quarrel, but nothing can prevent the Vicar and myself from coming to blows ultimately—about you know whom.'

'Do you love her so very, very much, then?' asked Prue, with tenderest insinuation. The next best thing to having the Curate in love with herself was to hear his confidence about another.

'Love!' cried Mr. Bacchus, firing up. 'I attach no meaning whatever to that word, it is too hackneyed. It does not meet my case in the least. I am being slowly envenomed, maddened, unhumanized—that is what I mean by being in love.'

'And is there no hope for you?' asked
Prue, her dovelike eyes brimming over with
fondest solicitude.

'Exactly as much as there is for any cross-
ing-sweeper at Piccadilly Circus. But there
is one comfort—at least, I feel it so. There
is no more chance for Mr. Meridian either.
If Miss Ivory ever said "yes" to him, I should
be ready to make an end of the Vicar or
myself, or both.'

'I hope not,' Prue said, her pious mind
shocked at such sentiments coming from the
lips of a clergyman. 'You would do nothing
wrong, I am sure.'

'Don't be too sure,' the Curate replied.
'I sometimes feel capable of crimes that
would make your hair stand on end, and the
worst—or the best—of it is, that no deeds,
however desperate, would mend matters in the
least. If Miss Ivory had as many suitors as
Penelope, and I slew them all, like Ulysses,
what good would it do?'

In spite of the exaggeration and bombast
of these speeches, it was easy to discern the

depth of passion underneath. To the Curate a great grief or a painful discontentment came as to a child. All the world must know, all the world must be in sympathy with him.

'You see,' he went on, 'folks may say what they like. There is no one else, search the world over, in the least like Miss Ivory: so natural—in spite of beauty that would turn any other girl's head—so clever, and so kind. She cannot bear to hurt the feelings of a fly, and I am about of as much importance as a fly in her eyes. If she were to smash me against the window and have done with it, I am sure I should be grateful. Things are not even in this life : you must have noticed that. If a man is without one thing, he is without a dozen. If he has a dozen things, he is sure to have a hundred. There is no law of compensation——'

Prue again looked slightly reproachful, but let him go on.

'Now is there ?' asked Mr. Bacchus. 'I ask you, is there any law of compensation ? Take my own case. I am a half-starved

Curate, eking out existence on a hundred a
year. A beautiful wife and a large fortune
would make up for everything. But I shall
never get one—I mean, I shall never get
Miss Ivory ! Then look at Mr. Meridian.
He enjoys every advantage life can give.
They say he is sure to be made a bishop one
day. He won't get Miss Ivory—the Lord
be praised!—but a dozen handsome girls with
fortunes, and I dare say titles, would have
him to-morrow if he asked them. Well, don't
let us harp any longer on these maddening
topics. It is quite settled, then. We are all
to keep house together.'

His attitude changed suddenly from morbid
depression and apathetic despair to alert cheer-
fulness.

'Your fortune will permit of quite an
establishment. The first thing to see about,
therefore, is a suitable house. I have one
in my mind. Then we must look after cook,
parlour-maid, gardener, and the like. And
that reminds me. There is a tip-topping
cook just out of place at Holmdale. I

had better go and engage her for you at once.'

'Would it not be more prudent to wait a little, till we see what we get?' Prue said timidly.

'You are sure, anyhow, to want a cook. Still, the house is the most important question to settle. If you don't mind putting on your bonnet, we could go this very moment and look at that pretty place with a lodge just outside the village, now to let.'

'There can be no harm in looking at it,' Prue replied, delighted to see his changed humour.

'Then by all means let us go,' was the eager reply. 'I know the agent, and a very gentlemanly, pleasant fellow he is. He has given me a lift in his gig many a time. A hint from me, and I am sure he would keep the place open for you.'

They set off, and the inspection proved quite satisfactory. Had they built a house for themselves, they could not have contrived one more suitable and convenient, said the

Curate. The grounds were delightful, too ; the coachhouse and stabling all that could be desired. Then there were reception-rooms, and bedchambers sufficient for the accommodation of a family-party twice as large as their own—in fact, everything was in accordance with an income of five thousand a year.

' I have made up my mind that your share will amount to that,' said the delighted Mr. Bacchus. ' It really cannot be less. And if we get in at once, it would not be too late for a garden-party, the very thing by way of inauguration. I will write out a list of invitations the first thing on reaching home.'

Pleased to see him pleased, poor Prue made a show of enthusiasm, though her heart sank within her. She was in the same predicament as himself. The visionary five thousand a year touched her imagination coldly, but had the Curate asked her to share his poverty— ah ! that would have been rapture, something to her advantage indeed.

CHAPTER VIII.

MRS. DE ROBERT TAKES TO HER BED.

IF the sight of the Wooden Horse struck awe into the souls of the beleaguered Trojans, still deeper was the effect wrought on Mrs. de Robert's mind by the van-load of treasure as, under police escort, it slowly wound its way to the Manor.

We are not told that the Trojans took to their beds, but such was the plight to which Mrs. de Robert was reduced by that portentous spectacle. She had a way of taking to her bed whenever things went wrong; and a very comfortable way it is for all concerned. If we could all take to our beds till the moment of perturbation is over—be it ill-temper, low spirits, a worrying fit, or any other abnormal humour—how much easier everyday life would become ! As a rule, people nowadays do not spend nearly enough time in bed. We air our worries abroad too much. We are not sufficiently ashamed of being uncomfortable.

Mrs. de Robert was certainly a superior person in this respect. She did take pains to keep out of everybody's way when everybody was odious to her—except Miss Ivory, of course. Never was her belief in Eugenia more delightful to witness than during these crises. The young lady would straightway don the most charming little bib and apron in the world, and hover about the sick-room, plying her patient with mutton-broth and jelly—in fact, treating her exactly as if she were suddenly stricken down with ague or rheumatism.

'Are you better, Roberta?' she would say, in a voice of affectionate solicitude. At the same time she was not beguiled with the least dissimulation. She never minced matters, or

called Mrs. de Robert's indisposition by fictitious names. The bouts of ill-humour were
so many ailments, to be nursed, physicked,
and got rid of.

'Just think!' Mrs. de Robert said, when the
sharpness of the attack had been in some
measure subdued by this judicious treatment;
'these Murillys and curiosities might have
made a fine show for us at Bath or Brighton.
We could have given entertainments to all
the celebrities who visited the place. We
should have been so looked up to, so well
thought of!'

'After all,' Eugenia said as she stood by
the sick-bed, gruel-basin in hand, 'we could
not have taken this van-load with us on our
travels. It is really a far greater worry to
have curiosities than not to have them. You
can neither eat, drink, nor wear them; but
there they are, filling up room, in everybody's
way, a perfect nuisance to housemaids.'

'There is something in that, Eugenio,' was
the reply from the night-capped patient
reposing in the curtained four-poster; 'and if

only decent folks had come after them, I
should have been the last person in the world
to utter a murmur.   I wanted to be rid of
the rubbish.   I wanted to be free to roam
about the world like Moll Flanders and
Peregrine Pickle.   But to think that so much
as a farthing's worth of my poor Affie's property should go to a rapscallion lot like this
—a double-faced, thumbscrewing Jesuit ; a
couple of Mormons with who knows how
many wives left at home ; and two cheese-
paring old maids.   No, Ivey ; I shall never
get over it as long as I live—never, never.'

'In one sense you will get over it,' said the
ever-ready comforter.   ' You won't have to
do it again.'

' You are right there,' Mrs. de Robert
replied, with more energy.   ' Tell Mr. Meridian
to make haste, then.   Never, I do honestly
believe, was such a man for dawdling.   The
things have come ; the people are here.   Why
on earth should he shilly-shally in this
exasperating fashion ?   He has had time to
settle the business a dozen times over.'

'Who knows but that this delay may turn out the greatest possible blessing; at the eleventh hour the very person you have desired coming forward and claiming the property!'

'I wish he would, I am sure. Nothing would please me better than to send these people about their business. It would exactly serve them right. What could that scatter-brain—Lord forgive me!—what could my poor darling have been thinking about when he left me such a job as this? True enough, I proposed it myself. I thought it would make him so comfortable in his grave. And this worry is all I get for my pains.'

'But a good deal of agreeable conversation: you forget that,' put in Eugenia.

'Humph!' said Mrs. de Robert, with her little rasping laugh. 'You would get agreeable conversation out of a gate-post on those terms! However, I am glad if the whole thing has amused you, Jenny.'

'Immensely!' Miss Ivory answered. 'I can afford to like these good people, you see.

They have nothing to get out of me. I must
say I think them quite above the ordinary
run. There is the Jesuit father, for instance.
Put the thumbscrew, Galileo, and Joan of Arc
out of your mind, and can you imagine a
more entertaining, delightful talker ! And so
distinguished—every inch a gentleman.'

'He entertained me vastly before I knew
who he was, I must say,' Mrs. de Robert
said.

'And after all,' Miss Ivory added, pursuing her advantage, 'the thumbscrew, Galileo, or Joan of Arc have nothing more to do
with him than you and I have to do with the
two little princes smothered in the Tower.
I don't suppose he would himself tread on a
worm.'

'He seems a mild, kind-hearted, gentlemanly old fellow, certainly,' was the reply.

'As to his Jesuitical ways,' continued the
young lady, 'there can be no real harm in
teaching poor savages to leave off eating each
other and cover their nakedness. At any rate,
they are no worse off than they were before.'

'True enough that,' Mrs. de Robert said, as she reposed on her pillows.

'Then, again, supposing—I am only supposing—that anybody gave him a beautiful picture, say by Murillo or any other celebrated painter. It seems to me the South Sea Islanders want it much more than we English people do.'

'Poor innocents, yes,' was the answer.

'And with regard to the two Mormons, as you call them,' Miss Ivory went on, 'they seem as good and kind as can be. If each has a dozen wives and makes all happy, it surely speaks volumes in their favour! How many husbands do not take the trouble even to please one!'

'You are right there,' Mrs. de Robert cried, quite cheerfully.

'The fact of having no money, either, is surely not to be assumed to their discredit,' Eugenia added. 'We can never be sure how people come by their large fortunes; but one thing we may be sure of—when we find them without, they are not living on fraud and spoliation.'

'On my word, that is just what I feel,' was the answer. ' I was never fond of money-getting folks myself. The pair of Yankees are honest enough, I'll be bound.'

'It is, on the whole, much pleasanter to give money or anything else to those who want it, than to those who have too much already. What would you have said at the sight of a Frankfort Jew or a Levantine usurer?'

'I believe it would have been the death of me. I always hoped poor dear Affie's property would comfort some poor soul in distress.'

'Which it certainly will do,' Eugenia said coolly. 'A fourth part, a sixth of the money will be comparative wealth to the two ladies ; whilst the rest equally divided——'

'Don't talk of it,' Mrs. de Robert said. 'I'm like the folks who like to fancy themselves a-dying. When there seems any chance of it, they would take all the drugs in an apothecary's shop to get well again. Oh dear, oh dear! why can't people take their belongings with them? Who would have thought Affie's whim would prove such a plague to me ?'

'You will be better soon,' Eugenia said soothingly. 'And the sooner the better— for me.'

'Yes, I want to get well for your sake, Jenny. We'll be gadding about then some-where. But here I am, easy and comfortable in my bed, and here I mean to stay till the business is over.'

'Will you have a cup of arrowroot by-and-by?' asked Eugenia, with fond solicitude; 'or a little tea and toast? that, I think, would not hurt you.'

'Just what you please. Give me anything you like,' Mrs. de Robert said; 'only don't let Mr. Meridian come to bother me.'

'He shall bother me instead,' was the suave reply; 'and of course, Roberta, he won't expect to see you till you are well enough to be downstairs again. Even Mr. Meridian would not ask an audience of you in your night-cap!'

'I shan't go downstairs till the van-load is

unpacked, and the people sent about their business,' said the invalid, turning her head on the pillow for a comfortable nap.

Miss Ivory, perceiving the Vicar at the garden-gate, hastened downstairs just as she was—and well did that pretty white nursing-apron become her.

'How is Mrs. de Robert this afternoon?' asked the visitor, in the most matter-of-fact way.

'Rather better, thank you,' Eugenia replied, as gravely as possible.

It was not the first occasion on which the Vicar had made such inquiries. Mrs. de Robert's singularities were tolerably familiar to him by this time, and he humoured them, or at any rate ignored them, when politeness required. An old writer defines a philosopher as what is meant by a gentleman, and certainly there is a kind of philosophy which may better be described as good manners than anything else.

'Will she be downstairs to-morrow, think you?' again he asked.

'I fear not; but it depends upon circumstances. When is the unpacking to begin?'

The Vicar looked at Eugenia. Eugenia looked at the Vicar.

'Not till the last moment,' he said; adding mysteriously: 'You don't suppose, do you, that Mrs. de Robert would part with any of her treasures after having once more enjoyed the sight of them? They must be kept out of her sight—spirited away. But I have arranged everything. Trust to my management.'

'If you cannot manage the business, no one can; and I am sure you will satisfy everybody,' said Eugenia.

'The question—from Mrs. de Robert's point of view, at least—is not to satisfy these good people, but to get rid of them,' the Vicar said, with a touch of malicious satisfaction, the image of the epigrammatic Doctor rising before him. 'And got rid of they shall be. I promise that. Before another week is over, not a fraction of the treasure, not a claimant, shall be left in the place.'

'Unless others appear at the eleventh hour ?'

'I have provided against that emergency,' was the prompt reply. 'One sixth part is to be retained for a certain period in case of such tardy applications being made. Failing this, it will be divided among the rest.'

'And is the money to be equally portioned out ?' asked Miss Ivory, sympathetically anxious.

'You will see when the time comes,' he said, in the same quick, decided tones. 'As Mrs. de Robert has now left every detail to me, it is advisable to keep my own counsel. Were you put in possession of my programme she would ferret it out, and insist on inter- fering at the eleventh hour. The entire business would then have to be begun over again. But do persuade her to show herself at the ceremony of distribution. Otherwise it will be seen that she really begrudges the gifts.'

Eugenia did not look very hopeful on that score.

'After all,' the Vicar said, as if a sudden thought had struck him, 'it really does not much matter. Let her stay in bed, then, till the dreadful transaction is over. Let her do exactly as she pleases. Indeed, my errand now was with yourself rather than with her. What I wanted to say was this. You are virtually the lady of the house ; you are the real mistress here. You hinted the other day at something in the shape of an entertainment to close up the proceedings ?'

'Mrs. de Robert should surely show her relations a little hospitality before final departure ?' Eugenia said.

'By all means. I quite approve of the notion. Make your own arrangements, then, and I will do my best to help you,' the Vicar replied cheerfully and pleasantly.

These repeated interviews with Eugenia might result in nothing, but they made him feel cheerful and pleasant at the time. Her friendliness was perhaps no more meant especially for him than the sunshine; for all that, like the sunshine, it warmed his heart.

As usual, he had a little passage of arms with her before parting.

'You might do worse than turn yourself into a hospital nurse,' he said, looking at the white bib apron. 'Such an example would prove contagious. You would thus become heroic vicariously, as well as in the fact.'

She laid aside her apron somewhat sadly. The sarcasm jarred.

'I suppose I am like a good many other women,' she replied. 'I would be heroic if I could.'

He also became suddenly serious.

'You cannot say that you have no chances in that line,' he said, for the life of him unable to keep silent. 'What truer heroism than to sacrifice one's own happiness for that of another? Such an opportunity, at least, is yours.'

CHAPTER IX.

T may readily be supposed that the police-escorted van exhilarated all concerned but Mrs. de Robert. Sabina's gentle hopes, Prue's meek anticipations, were, however, all outdone by the enthusiasm of their partners in good fortune. The behaviour of the good Priest was consistent. Having made up his mind to obtain possession of the Murillo and a certain pair of branched silver candlesticks he had heard of, he quietly set to work to talk Mr. Meridian over. Every day for the space of a week he paid a little visit to the Vicarage in order to continue negotiations. The discussion began

and ended with the Murillo and the silver
candlesticks, no other topics appearing of
sufficient importance to be even mooted. To
compare small things with great, those daily
conversations were like the historic wrangle of
Thiers and Bismarck over Strasburg and
Metz. Which of the two would win his
cause? What would be the fate of Strasburg
and Metz—in other words, of the Murillo and
the silver candlesticks?

The Vicar was a deep man, and more than
a match for the most Jesuitical Jesuit going.
There was, indeed, a considerable leaven of the
Jesuit in his composition. It was not in the
least difficult to him to conceal his thoughts,
except when with the distracting Miss Ivory;
and over his tongue, also, he exercised easy
sway. If he did not wish to disclose any
especial fact, no one on earth could make him
disclose it. Thus the reverend father was
always received in the most cordial, concilia-
tory spirit, and always heard with extreme
deference, but he never got an inch nearer the
truth.

So instructive were the long talks on Spanish art that Mr. Meridian ought to have admitted the more artistic of his parishioners to hear them. He was himself a man of wide reading, also a traveller; in this especial field, however, neither knowledge nor experience could bear comparison with those of his visitor. He had never set foot on Spanish soil, and who can speak authoritatively of Murillo without a journey to Seville?

The Priest was fresh from a residence in Spain. He had every particular concerning the Spanish master—bibliographical, historic, statistical—at his fingers' ends, so that his discourses abounded with knowledge. Very dexterously and plausibly he allowed the main point—in other words, the ultimate fate of Mrs. de Robert's great canvas—to remain wholly in the background. In glowing terms he descanted upon the characteristics of the painter, the merits of this masterpiece and that; in fine, he spoke so learnedly and feelingly that Mr. Meridian, or anyone else interested in the subject, could have listened to

him all day long. The perusal of a dozen
works on art in general, or on Murillo in particular, would not have instructed him in anything like the same degree. Then he brought
prints and photographs to help out his de-
scriptions, till Seville and its pictorial treasures
seemed to rise before the listener. Touchingly
insinuative, too, he would recall laborious days
spent by himself under the warm Andalusian
heavens; dwell upon the consolations that
beauty, alike natural and ideal, had afforded
him; and with tears in his eyes describe some
especial mood of religious fervour, when, kneel-
ing in rapt ecstasy at the foot of a Murillo,
heaven itself had seemed to open to his
vision.

'I assure you, my dear sir,' he said one day,
after an unusually long and agreeable sitting,
'the deep interest I take in this family heir-
loom, and the positive rapture with which the
bare possibility of possessing it fills my heart,
are beyond my power to describe. Possessing
it, did I say? You and I, priest and priest,
may well disclaim motives that do no dis-

honour to other men. We covet, but not for ourselves, not for earthly children, living testimonies of fireside love and joy ; instead, for those helpless and nameless ones who may be classed under one general head—the orphan-hood of humanity. You are at one with me here, and, indeed, on how many other vital questions! The partition wall that divides us is thin indeed! You can realize the ardent, nay, painful craving I feel for this treasure ; yet, after all, what matters its destination, provided it adorns some building consecrated to God; provided it brings the callous to their knees, the carnal-minded to penitence! Never was enthusiasm more needed ; never genius more in request as a ministrant of religion than in these days. I beseech you, therefore, whatever you do, let not your Murillo fall into worldly hands ; let it not furnish vain gratification to the sensual and the self-indulgent, prove one drop more in the cup already brimful of luxury and mammon.'

This eloquent appeal, like the rest of its predecessors, left the matter very much where

it was ; and at the close of the seven days'
parley, the discouraged father felt no surer of
obtaining his end than at the beginning.   It
really seemed to him that Mr. Meridian
wanted the Murillo and the candlesticks for
himself.   Such might reasonably be the case,
supposing a claim of kinship could be put in.
The Vicar of Hopedale was inclined to High
Church doctrines ; candles had appeared long
ago on the altars of neighbouring churches—
any Sunday the same innovation might greet
the eye of Hopedale folk.

Nevertheless, the Priest did not relax his
efforts.   The visits went on, the parleyings
went on ; and but for the decisive day at
hand, it seemed as if they might go on for
ever.

The other claimants held modestly aloof,
Mr. Meridian being wholly unmolested as far
as the quartette were concerned.   Truth to
tell, the whole affair now wore a different
aspect in the eyes of nephew and uncle.   It
was less the much-dreamed-of heritage they
aspired after, than the hand of the incom-

parable Miss Ivory. Unselfish here, as under
all other circumstances and conditions, the elder
Derrober entered heart and soul into the feelings of the younger. Material interests were
merged in questions of far deeper import, or
only dwelt upon as they might affect them.
Would Miss Ivory dream for a moment of
accepting a man who had nothing but himself
to offer? The two discussed the subject as
untiringly as the father and Mr. Meridian
had talked over the Murillo and the silver
candlesticks.

It was highly characteristic of the pair that
they should thus lose sight of worldly
aggrandizement for the hundredth time in
life; shut their eyes to the something they
might hear of to their advantage.

Whilst the reverend father insinuated,
harangued, coaxed, and the ladies laid bare
their circumstances in every particular, these
two remained proudly reticent. Like Jason,
they had come in search of the Golden Fleece;
but having come, were at no pains to slay the
dragon. Even their schemes for the remodel-

ling of society were now in abeyance, the
Phalanstery eclipsed, the Golden Age lying
before us forgotten.

'I'll tell you what, nephew,' said Mr.
Derrober, with a look of conscious sagacity.
much as if he considered himself the personification of worldly wisdom, just indeed what
he was not. 'I'll tell you the long and the
short of it, my boy. There is but one way
for an honest man to deal with a true woman.
Speak out.'

The Doctor, who possessed plenty of wis-
dom, but rather that of Rabelais than of
Poor Richard, pondered before making reply.
When he did speak, it was hardly to cut the
Gordian knot.

'My respected uncle,' he said, arching his
eyebrows, 'now, do tell me, are you a pre-
historic lake-dweller come to life again, or a
vivified citizen of the age of bronze? You
speak like these. Don't you know that the
woman of the olden time is a survival—a
heroine obsolete as Lot's wife? The course
you propose might have answered when the

world was in its bib and pinafore; but times have changed since then, and woman too. The nineteenth-century paragon is a very complex creature, no more to be compared to her forerunner than the vertebrate to the jelly-fish.'

' Miss Ivory is not a bit of a blue-stocking,' replied the other comfortably.

' Oh, as if algorithms and the Greek particle, had anything to do with it! Aptitudes and superiorities are born with us, in the blood. We suck 'em in with mother's milk.'

' But you are a man of no mean parts, Frank. You have as much knowledge and experience as most of your fellows. No woman need be ashamed of you when you open your lips, I am sure.'

The Doctor shook his head.

' My good sir, just put my parts in the scales with Miss Ivory's aspirations, and see which would kick the beam. I feel sure of it; a girl of her spirit and character has horizons wide as those of an Alpine panorama.

Nothing short of a career would satisfy her.'

'When did honest, faithful love fail to satisfy a woman?' said the elder.

'Back to the cave you issued from, with your flint carving-knives and mammoth-bones! My respected uncle, you are a hundred, hundreds of years behind your time. Don't you know that love, as you call it, is as completely out of date as troubadours and Court-fools? Instead of seeking leafy solitudes and haunts of the nightingale, lovers nowadays solve algebraic problems in company, or get up statistics of crime by way of courtship. This finished creature wants worthy surroundings. The frame must match the picture. She should marry a man of means.'

'She has, doubtless, an ample fortune of her own,' said the elder, after a pause. 'And you are pretty sure to get something from our kinswoman. Women, moreover, are very generous when they have once given their affections. And'—here he hesitated, and got out, with much feeling and a touch of sadness—'if, indeed, things turn out well for you, my lad, we will let other considerations go, and leave the betterment of the world to your children. What's mine is yours, you know. 'Tis little enough an old fellow like myself wants when once he parts company with schemes for benefiting humanity.'

The Doctor might have passed for a man without feelings, so skilfully did he conceal them now. The eyes of the other, however, filled with tears as he replied, for he knew well that the words came from the depth of his heart.

'Tush, tush!' he said; 'you ought to be ashamed of yourself to put such base thoughts into my head. Why, to deprive you of pocket-money for turning the world topsy-turvy would be about as inhuman as to bury you alive. No, old curmudgeon! you shall ride your hobby-horses like a prince yet; and I'll ride with you when this last has kicked me off. It may not be written in the stars that Miss Ivory is to marry the Honourable and Reverend Mr. Meridian, and in due time become a bishop's lady. But she will never marry Frank Derrober, that's positive.'

'Not unless Frank Derrober ask her,' said the other gently.

'Now, sir, did you ever ask a woman and get a refusal? Answer me.'

'I have gone through an ordeal more painful still. I have been asked by a noble woman, and had to refuse her.'

'Why could you not accept?' asked the Doctor, evidently pondering on the matter. The reply came after some hesitation.

'She was rich. I had not a dollar to call my own. I felt that I should be weighed down by a sense of perpetual obligation.'

'Humph! the moral is à propos,' the Doctor said drily.

'By no means. My case differed essentially from your own. I was not in love.'

'Well,' replied the other more cheerfully, 'we'll see. I may feel quite differently this

day se'nnight. Five thousand pounds before
now have worked miracles. Ten have all but
made the sun stand still. Twenty might turn
me into a proper gentleman, a presentable
character. And mighty pleasant such a condition of expectancy. But for glorious hopes,
like these, soap-bubbles that burst, who
would give a jackstraw for this paltry
life!'

With that philosophic reflection the Doctor
left off talking about Miss Ivory, which was
not quite the same thing as to leave off thinking about her. That would indeed have been
difficult just now. Every day they met, and
every day under circumstances that rendered
her more adorable. Eugenia was, indeed, doing
her utmost to atone for Mrs. de Robert's
unfriendly attitude. Perhaps grave doubts
assailed her as to the final issue of this
business.

She could never feel quite sure of her old
friend when it came to a crisis. So as the
Doctor's behaviour was circumspection itself,
after the half-confession of a few days back,

and as his conversation was livelier and more engaging than ever, she performed her duties of hostess, and yielded freely to the charm.

CHAPTER X.

MRS. DE ROBERT'S HOBGOBLINS.

AS the eventful day drew near, Mrs. de Robert's illness took an aggravated form. She certainly did not as yet refuse nourishment, or manifest any of those grave symptoms that alarm anxious relations. Her condition, whilst not dangerous, was nevertheless as bad as well could be. Miss Ivory, serenity itself, betrayed nothing in the sick-room, but out of it could not conceal her uneasiness. What if at the eleventh hour a stop should be put to all proceedings? what if, after all, the unhappy questors after something to their advantage should be sent away empty-handed and resentful? Hitherto

she had scouted such a notion when suggested
to her by the Vicar. Now she felt obliged .to
acknowledge the same ground for apprehen-
sion; and the provoking part of the business
was that Mr. Meridian seemed to have turned
round. He would go his own way, turning a
deaf ear to her misgivings.

Was it—no, she would not, could not believe
this of Mr. Meridian—yet the question would
arise, was it that he was thus pursuing his
way bent on mischief? Long ago he had fore-
told a dismal fiasco to the little drama. Was
he well pleased to have his words made good?
The next moment she reproached herself for
the unworthy suspicion. He was outwardly
cold, a trifle hard, and given to self-estimation ;
he was, for all that, incapable of double-dealing.
She felt it, nevertheless, her duty to warn
him.

'If Mrs. de Robert refuses to divide the
property among her friends, I shall feel I
ought to give them mine!' she said, with
heightened colour, and almost with tears of
vexation. ' Think of the distance they have

come, the hopes they have been allowed to cherish for so long; the boon, too, that anything in the shape of fortune would be to all.'

He looked at her with an odd provocative smile. Was not this attitude of a piece with the inconsequence of womankind? Hitherto, who so confident as herself, who so deaf to his hints of a catastrophe? Now he supposed, just out of contrariety, and from a spirit of contradiction, she was ready to cry with dismay.

'You shall be under no necessity of bestowing your fortune——' 'even upon the epigrammatic Doctor,' was on his lips; he refrained, and added, 'whatever you may do of your own free will. I flatter myself my strategy is more than a match for our old friend's temper. Besides, she has virtually handed over the property in trust to me. Am I likely to surrender it?'

Miss Ivory did not look quite reassured.

He went on, still quite confident:

'For diseases like this of Mrs. de Robert, we must have recourse to drastic remedies. She has laid upon me a duty; that duty I shall discharge, no matter what obstacles she may put in my way.'

'It is not so much the money that her mind harps upon,' Eugenia said, still unconvinced and uneasy. 'She has enough and to spare of her own. But I am sorry she ever promised to transfer her family heirlooms during her lifetime. She seems to cling to them now.'

'She cannot very well carry them to that paradise in Central Africa you intend to visit—to Bongo,' Mr. Meridian said jestingly. 'You would both certainly be murdered for sake of the spoil—which I wonder you are not here, by the way. Does not the thought of harbouring so much treasure prevent you from sleeping?'

Eugenia was ruffled and vexed. The Vicar's banter jarred just then.

'I wish I had nothing else to keep me awake,' she answered with pique. 'However, as you can move mountains, and cause rivers to flow backwards, I ought to feel ashamed of myself for being uneasy at all. So, then, I may cast my fears to the winds. To-morrow you will conjure Mrs. de Robert out of her bed, put her in the best possible humour, and dismiss the claimants, one and all, enriched and delighted?'

'Yes, I think I can promise you so much,' he replied coolly. 'I fear yours is but an uncomfortable time of it in our old friend's room. This perpetual hankering after the impossible must try your nerves ;' and, as he said this, he looked at her kindly and anxiously.

'I know Mrs. de Robert too well to take her humours to heart,' Eugenia answered ; 'and it is ever other people she finds fault with, not myself.'

'That is an element of comfort, certainly. I dare say I come in for my full share of abuse. However, Mrs. de Robert and I understand each other pretty well by this time ; and let her say what she will, we are fast friends at bottom. Well, present my gift, and say I hope she will be feeling well enough to join us in the morning.'

Mr. Meridian had brought the invalid some luscious figs, the choicest product of his garden. Daintily cradled in leaves, and placed in a pretty rustic basket, the offering looked the most appetizing imaginable.

'Only look at what Mr. Meridian has sent you!' Eugenia said cheerfully as she entered the sick-room, basket in hand. 'Did you ever behold more delicious figs?'

Mrs. de Robert sat up in bed and eyed the Vicar's offering with ill-concealed satisfaction. She was bound to feel displeased at everything, but she adored green figs.

'Humph!' she said. ' 'Tis a pity he didn't put a viper inside. 'Twould have come in handy, for I feel just ready to make away with myself.'

'You will eat a fig, nevertheless,' said Eugenia gravely, as she picked out the largest and ripest.

'Oh, Ivey! Ivey!' cried Mrs. de Robert, 'what an arrant fool I have been! If you could see the fruit-basket of frosted silver packed up in one of those cases, you would feel, like me, ready to cry your eyes out. 'Tis a little gem, so chaste, so elegant, you would see nothing prettier on her Majesty's table.'

'Never mind, Roberta ; we will buy some antique silver, you and I between us. And just think of the pleasure of having and using what is our very own !'

'I'm mighty glad I told Affie I should keep the things on the sideboard—the tea-service and snuffers,' Mrs. de Robert went on maliciously. 'I shall keep a thing or two more, in spite of Mr. Meridian. See if I don't ! He is not going to have it all his own way this time.'

She took another morsel of her fig, and continued almost in a whisper :

''Tis all very well to prate about death-bed promises, and the like. But whatever I promised my poor darling—ah, one must die to be a darling ! I am always saying that—whatever I promised my poor darling, nothing was said as to time. I was free to use the things and enjoy the things as long as I

pleased.   What he cared about was that one
of his family should possess them ultimately.
Now, Eugenio, I'm not going to be unhand-
some; I'm not going to distribute soup-
tickets, and then turn a host of starving
creatures from my door.   Oh no; I'll be
square, as true as my name is Sarah Roberts!
But just put your ear down, Ivey.   I really
can't part with the things in the cases yet—
the Murilly and the silver basket, and such
like.   It makes me bad to think of it.   I
shall just stay patiently in my bed till I hear
the carpenters at work below, and then I shall
go downstairs and plump myself on the first
case they attempt to meddle with; and that's
what I mean to do, and no one on earth shall
prevent me!'

Miss Ivory said nothing, but her look dis-
commended.   The bare notion of such a
scandal shocked her inexpressibly.   The scene
rose before her mind's eye : Mr. Meridian pre-
siding, the happy claimants blissful and expectant; and rushing into their midst, dashing
all hopes to the ground, the wild figure of

Mrs. de Robert in dressing-gown and night-cap. She was capable of carrying out her threat, and something more.

'You have never seen the things, or you would feel as I do,' Mrs. de Robert went on insinuatingly. 'It would take me a week to describe 'em. You see, they are not all family belongings. My poor Affie had a craze for Apostle spoons and George the Third teapots, and whatever he could lay hands on he marked with the *fleur de lis.* 'Tis all of a piece, he would say; and so long as it has belonged to one of the name, 'twill answer the same purpose as if it had descended from generation to generation. Oh, why did he not marry me when I was a younger woman! I've no fondness for babies, nasty squalling brats—poor dear innocents! But you know what I mean. Had poor Affie had a child of his own, all this botheration would have been spared me. I might have enjoyed the things in peace.'

'Well,' Eugenia said cheerfully, 'as you cannot enjoy them in peace, it will be much better to have them out of your sight.'

'But to think that the Murilly and the
silver candlesticks will go to the Pope and the
Inquisition, as I am sure they will! Mr.
Meridian is mum; and when he chooses to be
mum, you might as well shake an empty sack
expecting potatoes to drop out, as try to get
a scrap of information out of him. He's a
Jesuit in disguise himself, I'll be bound.
That's what all our clergy are coming to.
Then to think of these Mormons. Next to
a thumbscrewing Jesuit, I do think the
person I most detest is a man with seven
wives.'

' Nay,' Miss Ivory remonstrated very justly;
' it seems that neither of these gentlemen
possesses one wife, much less seven.'

' Oh, what won't men say to make their
story good! There is something wrong about
them, or they would never have crossed the
Atlantic on such an errand as this. If not
Mormons, be sure they are Fenians in disguise,
sent over to assassinate the Queen, or blow up
the House of Commons. They have a mighty
evil look, I can tell you; and we may say

what we like, but it's not genteel to be poor
—never was. Hark ! was not that a carpenter's tap ?'

'It is only the cook undoing a case of
wine. We had none in the house, so I
ordered some.'

'Are you quite sure ?' Mrs. de Robert
said, sitting up in her bed and listening
attentively.

'Quite positive. Indeed, Mr. Meridian has
the key of the lumber-room with him at the
Vicarage.'

That answer seemed to reassure the patient.
She settled herself once more comfortably on
her pillows.

'The sound of a hammer on these cases
would be as bad as if I heard nails being
driven into my own coffin,' she said. 'Worse,
I do think. But when to-morrow comes, you
will see, I shall do as I say. I'm not going
to have poor dear Affie's silver made into
graven images for Papists to worship, nor
pay the expenses of a second gunpowder plot.
As to the two harmless old maids, I bear

them no malice. They are as good as myself,
and a trifle better, I dare say. Mr. Meridian
may give them just whatever he pleases.
But it is of no use. Their names will die
with them. Like me, they are but a couple
of leafless boughs. Humph! these figs are
first-rate. The Vicar is vastly civil on a
sudden.'

Meantime all was bustle and preparation in
the lower regions of the Manor House. Not
only was wine being unpacked, but preparations for the more substantial part of the
banquet were carried on with the greatest
possible alacrity. Here Miss Ivory determined, at least, there should be no disenchant-
ment. However disastrously Mrs. de Robert
might interfere with the rest of the programme,
her reputation for hospitality should not be
allowed to suffer.

Like all girls of spirit, Miss Ivory delighted
in flutter and excitement. No sooner was
Mrs. de Robert in a comfortable drowse than
she flew to the pantry or the kitchen, donned
her housekeeping apron, and was forthwith

immersed in business. With the utmost relish she lent a helping hand to this one and that. Now she aided Lucy, the house-maid, to rub up glass and china. Now she whisked up syllabub or strained jelly, and all with a lightheartedness and ease that made such an auxiliary delightful to the servants.

'Oh, Sarah!' she said to the homely North-country woman who officiated as cook; 'how pleasant to have the house for once turned upside down! Why do people lead such dull, monotonous lives, when they might be bust-ling about like the show-folks getting ready for the fair?'

'Miss, as if I could answer such a question as that! You must go to the Scriptures,' was Sarah's cautious reply.

'Will the syllabubs be just perfection, think you?' again asked the young lady.

'Sure, miss, that is a bit riddlesome too. We does our best; but in small things as well as great, the Lord rideth the whirl-wind.'

'You mean that a thunderstorm to-night might turn the syllabub?' asked Miss Ivory anxiously.

'Lord, miss! That is what I ought to have meant, of course. But those who quote Scripture have said their say.'

CHAPTER XI.

MRS. DE ROBERT'S VOYAGE OF DISCOVERY.

MRS. DE ROBERT'S sleep was broken and uneasy that night. Again and again she woke up haunted by the sound of imaginary hammers. Another kind of nightmare that tormented her was a visionary encounter with the Vicar and the claimants. He had laid violent hands on the Murilly, the Jesuit aided and abetted, the Americans harangued, the ladies wept, and all was direst commotion. As soon as day began to break, she stole noiselessly out of bed, watched, and listened. All was hushed and silent. Evidently not a soul stirred. Miss Ivory slept in the next room, and not for worlds would she disturb her, but this suspense could be endured no longer.

Mrs. de Robert wanted to forestall Mr. Meridian, and also curiosity burned within her as to what that clever Eugenio had been about these last few days. She knew that nothing delighted Ivey so much as to turn the house topsy-turvy when she had a chance, and she felt sure that the delightful process had just been carried out with a vengeance. So, in night-cap and dressing-gown, tip-toe with expectation, Mrs. de Robert set forth on her prowl.

Hardly out of her bedroom, she stood still, dumfounded. The landing-place was transformed as if by magic. Tropical plants and flowers filled the large bay-windows; the well-worn stair-carpet was replaced by bright crimson baize. At intervals were placed baskets of ferns and begonias, whilst wax-lights in abundance occupied temporary brackets on the walls.

Mrs. de Robert made an odd grimace, divining Eugenia's little plot in a moment.

The monkey, thought Mrs. de Robert; she has invited the neighbours to a dance!

She continued her survey, sniffing surprise as she went. True enough, the drawing-room had been cleared for dancing, and was as festive as wreaths and garlands could make it. In the dining-room preparations were far advanced for the supper. Two long tables covered with finest damask, showed a glittering display of plate and crystal. Only the cut flowers and the regales were as yet wanting.

'Humph!' said Mrs. de Robert to herself. ' 'Tis mighty clever of Ivey to make every thing look so nice, I must say that; and now let us see what she is going to give her visitors to eat.'

She paused and listened. All remained still as before. Not a soul was astir. Then confidently, and with a look of extreme relish, she made her way to Eugenia's pantry. Here, indeed, was a sight to awaken enthusiasm in the mind of the least epicurean; but Mrs. de Robert had an uncommon liking for ballroom cates. Raised pies, whip-syllabubs and strawberry-creams ever put her in good temper.

When she glanced round at the tempting array of dishes, she quite forgot the mental disturbance of the last few days, as well as the nightmare from which she had just awakened, and complacently sat down to a little meal. The confinement to her room had ended in giving her an appetite. She could perhaps have eaten everyday fare in bed, had she tried. But she ever put a check upon her appetite during these attacks. Broth and gruel seemed more in accordance with the fitness of things.

But the revulsion of feeling now brought about, her amusement at the scale of Eugenia's preparations, above all the sight of a certain favourite dish, made her positively hungry. Having once more listened and assured herself that she was quite safe from observation, she whipped up a spoon, and with infinite relish attacked a dish of French flummery.

'Jenny will wonder what thief has been in her pantry,' she thought, chuckling over the escapade; 'well,' smacking her lips, 'there is plenty for folks to eat without the French flummery. 'Tis mighty good, I must say; just as we used to make it at home fifty years ago. Dear, how hungry I am, to be sure! I wonder if I can lay my hands on anything in the bread or biscuit way.'

She looked about, and succeeded in finding some old-fashioned, home-made rusks, that tasted uncommonly good with the flummery. Nothing indeed could be better; but now she must have something to drink as well.

'Lemonade—no, that's cold for this hour of the day. Humph! here's a little wine in a bottle: half a glass of Madeira won't hurt me, I'll be bound. But I believe that is Sarah lumbering overhead. I must be quick, or I shall be caught.'

Having by this time made an excellent meal, she drank her half-glass of Madeira—very warm and comforting it seemed under the circumstances—then hastened back to bed.

The retreat was effected only just in time ; a few minutes later, Sarah, the cook, descended, not, however, to go into the pantry and discover the depredations. Her business was in the dairy ; no one else would be downstairs for another hour to come.

Mrs. de Robert felt a wholly different creature when once more she laid her head on the pillow. The feverish discontent, the tormenting restlessness, alike the physical and mental discomfort from which she had lately suffered, now passed away. She felt soothed, refreshed, delightfully drowsy. In less than a quarter of an hour she was in a profound sleep, from which no carpenter's hammer downstairs would have aroused her.

When at last she awoke it was well-nigh noon. She sat up, looked round and listened. In spite of curtains and shutters, it was clear that she had slept a very long time ; in fact, that the day was already far advanced. Then the adventures of the night came back to her recollection, one by one : the tossing on a sleepless pillow ; the nightmare ; the surreptitious descent and discoveries made on the way; finally, that excellent little refection in the pantry.

She felt wonderfully alert now, and keenly alive to the excitement of the hour. The house was very silent, unnaturally so, she thought, for that time of the day. What could everybody be about? Mrs. de Robert loved mystification. She liked to surprise, and, although she would not for worlds have confessed it, she liked to be surprised in turn. The thing done, she rarely found fault with. The thing people proposed to do, was always in her eyes as bad as possible.

What could be going on now? Then, all at once, her old jealousy concerning the heirlooms came back. The carpenters had surely been at work whilst she slept. Mr. Meridian must be displaying her treasures to the assembled household; worse still, he was giving them away to the Pope, the Inquisition, and the men with seven wives apiece.

The thought was maddening. These good folks should have their money, and welcome.

But they should not have the Murilly and the plate and the jewels—no, not if her name was Sarah Roberts! Performing a make-shift toilette, as she had done a few hours before, she again went downstairs, peeping and listening by the way.

The dancing-room was deserted. The banquet-hall, as the drawing-room now deserved to be called, was empty also. Yet, as she advanced one step at a time, all her senses alive, she heard the well-known voice of Mr. Meridian. The sound proceeded from the breakfast-parlour, a small room opening on to the garden. Noiselessly and warily she approached the door, noting various facts by the way. On the hall-table lay several hats, the soft-felt head-gear of the Vicar and the Priest, the straw-hats of the Americans; she also observed some strange parasols, evidently the property of Selina Beckett and Patience Purfle.

She gathered, then, that the day's business had begun — the distribution was already taking place. Irritated at the bare thought of the business that had brought these visitors together, repenting more bitterly than before that she had ever decided to part with the property at all, feeling vindictive towards every one of those who had come forward to claim it, she was yet too much of a humorist not to relish the situation.

Mr. Meridian occupied a chair by the table, on which lay various papers and memorandum-books. On either side sat the claimants motionless as statues, suspense of a pleasurable kind written on every face.

There was pathos mingled with comedy in such a scene. Sabina and Prue had evidently been shedding tears of alternate hope and fear. They had taken off their bonnets which they twirled nervously on their laps, and both sat looking at Mr. Meridian as intently as prisoners gaze at their judges when brought up for sentence. Now they were red, now pale; depressed one moment, the next elated with ecstatic anticipation.

'Pray let us both expect the worst,' Sabina had said before setting out; 'as my Edwin

used to say—his words are engraven on my
memory—" Bina," he said, " if you want to keep
your mind in just equilibrium, always wake up
expecting the direst calamities that can afflict
humanity—the bank to break which holds
your little all, a good-for-nothing relation with
nine children to take up his abode with you,
Asiatic cholera to break out next door, or
your own house to be burnt to the ground.
These things, most likely, won't all happen at
once ; but by dwelling on the possibility of
such catastrophes we give the mind a healthy
tone." '

Opposite the pair sat the three men, the
place of honour next to Mr. Meridian being
occupied by the Priest.   He also testified the
liveliest interest in the proceedings, interest
by no means of impersonal kind.   He drew
out his pocket-handkerchief and replaced it,
hemmed and ha'd uneasily, bit his lips from
time to time, and glanced anxiously at the unreadable face of the umpire.

But the most curious study was that afforded
by the physiognomies of the uncle and nephew.

Whilst the elder Derrober behaved with the utmost impulsiveness, showing even more discomposure than the ladies and the priest, the Doctor sat with head erect and folded arms, the very personification of stoical indifference. A shipwrecked mariner in mid-ocean straining his eyes after some friendly sail, could hardly wear an intenser look than did the uncle. The nephew, on the contrary, was the personification of coolness, except when he glanced at the white-robed figure of Miss Ivory. Eugenia, dressed in muslin as befitted the season, sat a little removed from the group by the table. Wonderful to relate, her fingers were busy; she had on a chair beside her a basket of flowers, and was arranging them in bunches as she listened. No wonder that Dr. Derrober glanced that way. The slender, erect figure, the beautifully shaped head, the dark bright hair and fair face so hard to read, made a picture enchanting enough even to distract the attention of expectant next of kin at such a crisis.

Mr. Meridian looked much as he ever did—

circumspect, collected, entirely master of himself and the situation. Something, nevertheless, must have happened, thought the peeper
at the door. He was evidently about to make
an unexpected disclosure. As he manipulated
his papers and paused in his preamble, nothing
could be clearer than that he had surprises of
some kind or another for his little audience.
To Mrs. de Robert, spying at the key-hole, the
moment was as crucial as to the breathlessly
expectant claimants. If they were eager to
obtain possession of her treasures, still more
eager was she to keep them for herself.
Agape they all were, she knew well enough,
for the Murilly and the plate and the jewels ;
but for a brief interval, and by anticipation
only, was the joy of possession to be theirs.
How would they look when she broke in
upon them like a thunder-clap, and said her
say ?

She still paused at the key-hole, anxious to
learn what Mr. Meridian's preamble was all
about. Preamble it evidently was ; no one as
yet knew anything. Expectancy had reached

its acme, breathless suspense was at its height.

And, calmly and deliberately as if he were publishing the banns of marriage for half a dozen couples at church, the Vicar thus delivered himself :

' You have now, therefore, the preliminary facts before you. No legacy is here in question, as you have seen. The distribution of property is entirely a voluntary act on the part of Mrs. de Robert ; an act made in accordance, nevertheless, with the wishes of her late husband. It was his desire that, in case her own circumstances should so far alter in the future as to permit the sacrifice, she should seek out next of kin bearing his name, and hand over to them the money and family heirlooms, or as much of them as she felt ready to part with. Mrs. de Robert having entrusted me with the business from the beginning, I have endeavoured to act judiciously and impartially, and I hope and believe to the satisfaction of all concerned. I have now, however, to inform you that the delicate matter thus confided to me by my old friend has been simplified in an untoward, a mysterious, a most extraordinary manner.'

He glanced from one to the other of the little group, and got out in the same crisp, measured tones :

'To my great regret I have now to make known to you that the cases so carefully guarded, the cases to which no one here has had access but myself, are found to contain nothing but lumber. The family heirlooms of which you have all heard so much, the works of art, the plate and the jewels, have all vanished as completely as if the earth had swallowed them up !'

CHAPTER XII.

THE SECOND BOMBSHELL FALLS.

RS. DE ROBERT had heard more than enough. The piece of intelligence, awful to the expectant heirs as a thunder-clap, came welcome to her as a summer gale. It did more than relieve her of a grievous burden—it put her in the best possible humour, and made her feel years younger.

At first she could hardly believe in such a piece of good fortune. All difficulties in the way of a pacific settlement were now removed. She was relieved from the disagreeable duty of being churlish at the last moment. There would now be no squabbling over the treasure.

It was gone, and a mighty good riddance too.
The thumbscrewing Jesuit, the men with
seven wives apiece, the cheese-paring old
maids, might cry their eyes out to no purpose. The Murilly was providentially rescued
from the Pope or the Inquisition; the fruit-
basket of solid silver would not be melted
down by dynamiters sworn to blow up the
House of Commons; the jewels—well, they
might be put to good or bad uses, it was
no longer any business of hers. Anyhow,
there was an end of them as far as she was
concerned.

She forgot her nondescript toilette, for
toilette it was, in spite of the night-cap. She
was neither shoeless nor stockingless. Her
dressing-gown of bright-flowered stuff might
pass muster for a dress. Her cap was ornamented with lace frills and a lavender bow.
For that hour of the day, and in her own
house, she presented a very creditable appearance.

Indifferent to these considerations, she now
broke in upon the thunder-stricken company.

Hard as it was to these much-tried claimants to have the treasure wrenched from them at the last moment, it was harder still to lose the money. This terrible apparition in the night-cap could surely mean nothing else. The arbitress of Fate had changed her mind. One and all were to be sent away empty-handed as they had come. This something to their advantage had proved a mere Will-o'-the-wisp, an ignis fatuus luring to despair.

The lookers-on were characteristically affected. Miss Ivory, really frightened, rose from her seat with a little cry, her first thought being that Mrs. de Robert was either walking in her sleep, or a prey to mental hallucination. The epigrammatic Doctor, a moment before so apathetic, flew up like a Jack-in-a-box, and, careless of appearances, got behind Miss Ivory for protection and shelter.

Mr. Derrober raised his hands to heaven, as if entreating Divine pity under some cataclysmal visitation. The Priest whipped

out breviary and beads, and mumbled Pater-
nosters as fast as his tongue could go.

As to Sabina and Prue, they sat pale
as ghosts, holding each other's hands, and
trembling from head to foot. They were
like a pair of travellers surprised by a railway
accident, every moment expecting the very
worst.

Only Mr. Meridian maintained composure.
He certainly did not look as if the little
incident pleased him—quite the contrary.
He was evidently much disturbed, but no
more scared at Mrs. de Robert's unexpected
appearance than if a wasp had alighted on his
nose.

'An unexpected pleasure,' he said, smiling
satirically as he handed her a chair. 'Good-
morning, Mrs. de Robert. I hope I see you
well !'

'Good-day to you—and to you, sir—and you,
ma'am !' Mrs. de Robert said with the utmost
affability, making the tour of the room, and
giving her hand to each of the claimants by
turn. 'Well, Jenny, here I am ; but pray

don't let me interrupt. Pray go on!' she
added, addressing herself to Mr. Meridian; 'I
heard what you were just saying about the
Murilly and the plate and the rest.'

She glanced benignantly from one to the
other of the crest-fallen little audience.

'What can't be cured must be endured,'
she added airily. 'I am sure you were all
welcome enough to the rubbish. However,
'tis gone, and there's an end of it. We shall
not any of us, I'll be bound, live an hour the
less in consequence.'

She sat down beside Eugenia, Mr. Meridian
observing her with an odd expression. Her
whimsical behaviour did not seem to take him
very much by surprise. The rest of the
company regained composure by degrees. The
Doctor emerged from his hiding-place behind
Miss Ivory, patted his uncle encouragingly on
the shoulder, whispering, 'All right, old
fellow!' Sabina and Prue grew mildly cheerful by degrees, as folks on their way home
from a funeral. The Priest put away beads
and breviary. Order and composure being

perfectly restored, Mr. Meridian cleared his voice to begin again, keeping a sharp look-out on Mrs. de Robert all the time. In fact, he behaved much as a lion-tamer, who, whilst going through the day's performance, never once dares to take his eyes off some dangerous old animal.

'I've been the round of your pantry,' whispered Mrs. de Robert to Eugenia, 'and tasted your flummery, too. How good !' and she smacked her lips.

Eugenia smiled reprovingly. Mr. Meridian called to order in quick, rasping tones.

' Permit me to go on, Mrs. de Robert.'

'Pray go on,' she said ; 'I am sure that is just what I want you to do. You were saying——'

'The family heirlooms, then, of which I hold a carefully made out list in my hand, are unfortunately no longer in question—that is to say, not in question for the moment. It is to be hoped that we shall recover, at least, a portion of the missing property. The usual steps to that effect will of course be taken, and no exertions spared. Meantime, allow me to state that I had endeavoured to apportion these objects impartially, and with a view to the especial tastes and requirements of the recipients. The gem of the collection, the Murillo——'

'What is the good of making people's mouths water for nothing ?' broke in Mrs. de Robert. 'Much good it does to tell anyone you have given him something, which is no longer yours to give.'

'Permit me,' Mr. Meridian said severely. 'This beautiful work of art, a Holy Family by one of the greatest religious painters the world has ever known, was, without doubt, originally designed for a church. With what seems almost providential appropriateness, the Church sent one of its ministers to claim it. The Murillo, then—I feel sure, with the sanction of all present—I had set aside for the reverend father now among us.'

'I'd sooner see it burnt to tinder first,' whispered Mrs. de Robert audibly.

The Priest bowed melancholy acknowledgment. Mr. Meridian continued in the same inflexible tone.

'By whom it was to have graced some sacred edifice in a region but yesterday converted to civilization and Christianity.'

'Pretty Christianity that!' again Mrs. de Robert whispered audibly. 'The Inquisition, the rack, burnings in Smithfield, and the rest of it.'

'Will you permit me to continue?' asked Mr. Meridian, severer than before.

'I'm all attention,' Mrs. de Robert replied with affected meekness, the next moment whispering in Eugenia's ear, ''Twas the Jesuits that made Galileo swear the world didn't turn round; I know all about it.'

'Next in interest and value to this chef d'œuvre of Spanish art, came the armour,' Mr. Meridian proceeded. 'The collection contained some admirable specimens. After a good deal of deliberation, I felt it to be my duty to hand over these antiquities to our visitors from the New World.'

'Hear, hear!' cried the Doctor.

'It seemed to me, to say the least of it, as fitting an allotment as the first,' resumed Mr. Meridian. 'If an altar-piece painted by Murillo seemed a fitting donation to a Polynesian Cathedral, no less so were a suit of armour worn at Crécy or Poitiers to the museum of some infant city of the Far West.'

'Fiddle-de-dee!' murmured Mrs. de Robert. 'Haven't the Yankees got Red Indians and other antiquities of their own? And give me a good boiler or block-tin roasting-jack for all the armour in the world, I say.'

Mr. Meridian glanced sternly at his unruly client, and continued:

'I next had to dispose of the plate, old china, and jewellery; and here lay my greatest difficulty. The late Mr. de Robert desired— and very naturally, as it seemed to me—that the lion's share of his property should go to a male heir, some father of a family; in other words, he hoped that a claimant might come forward by whom the race and name would in all probability be continued. Such has

not been the case. Our visitors one and all are
celibates——'

'If that isn't enough to make poor Affie
turn in his grave, nothing will,' Mrs. de Robert
uttered aloud.

'It seems clearly my duty, under the circumstances, to keep back a portion, alike of
treasure and money, in reserve. The possibility of such a claimant coming forward at
the eleventh hour had to be provided
against.'

Here he glanced encouragingly at Sabina
and Prue.

'Of course compensation had to be made
to the ladies in money. I therefore proposed
to retain the rest of the heirlooms for the
present.'

'We'll make the round of all the pawn-
brokers' shops in London and ferret the things
out,' once more whispered Mrs. de Robert,
nudging Eugenia. 'I'm sure we deserve them
as much as any of 'em.'

'The result has shown that such a precau-
tion was by no means unnecessary,' continued

the Vicar, now contemptuously ignoring all
interruptions. 'Last evening, at a late hour, I
received a telegram from a sixth claimant
whose presence may daily, nay, hourly, be expected among us.'

This crowning surprise was too much even
for the circumspect Miss Ivory.

'Your genteel young man!' she whispered,
pressing her old friend's hand; 'I felt sure he
would come at the last.'

Mrs. de Robert's face beamed with exultation. She looked ready to embrace everybody
in the room.

The demeanour of the expectant heirs was
characteristic. The Doctor clapped his hands
as if he were at the play. His senior
looked resigned. The Priest, as if just told
by the dentist that the wrong tooth had
been pulled out. Sabina searched her memory
for some comfortable apothegm of the ever-
sapient Edwin. Prue wiped away a meek
tear.

'Under these circumstances,' Mr. Meridian
made haste to explain, 'it is expedient to

defer the final settlement of affairs. In the meantime,' here he glanced at the discomposed audience, ' pray be under no misapprehension. The claim, so late put in, will not be permitted to supersede others as valid, or materially to alter the disposition of the property.'

' I've a finger in that pie,' Mrs. de Robert whispered viciously.

' The subdivision may, however, have to be rearranged,' Mr. Meridian added. ' Some readjustment, some modification may be necessary——'

' I should just say so,' Mrs. de Robert murmured.

Not condescending to notice the offence, the Vicar went on :

' The newly-discovered member of the de Robert family possesses one qualification that, to say the least of it, emphasizes his claim——'

Just then a sudden commotion was heard throughout the house. Bells were rung impatiently. Doors flew open. The scurrying

feet and excited voices of domestics in hasty
conclave betokened some unusual event.

'This must be our expected visitor,' Mr.
Meridian said, looking at Mrs. de Robert and
Miss Ivory, as he put down his papers.

CHAPTER XIII.

IT were hard to say which of the two showed most curiosity, Mrs. de Robert or Miss Ivory, as they hurried out of the room to welcome the stranger. The elder lady's inquisitiveness, like the younger's, was tinged with romance. Whilst Eugenia perhaps expected to find some melancholy Ravenswood or imperious Rochester, Mrs. de Robert had evidently made up her mind that the new-comer was some dashing Peregrine Pickle, a harum-scarum to day, but to settle down in time the very model of a country gentleman. She had cherished the belief from the first that such

a claimant would come forward, carrying off
not only the family treasure, but the beautiful
Miss Ivory, her own Eugenio.

The two ladies made the best of their way
to the entrance-hall, which presented a scene
of pleasing confusion. A foreign atmosphere
reigned throughout the place. Snatches of
foreign speech reached their ears, outlandish
objects met their eyes—Oriental travelling gear,
brilliant rugs, bundles wrapt up in gorgeous
silk handkerchiefs, gaily ornamented baskets,
and an amount of nondescript luggage that
filled the place. Everything, indeed, savoured
of surprises. Instead of one stranger there
were two—two figures, at any rate, stood in
the doorway, both as romantic as if they had
been cut out of picture-books. The first, that
of a man of middle height, slender, with a
winning but somewhat anxious physiognomy,
advanced towards the ladies, pouring out
incomprehensible words of apology and explanation.

Now, as far as Mrs. de Robert and Eugenia
were concerned, the stranger's speeches might

just as well have been uttered in Hindostanee
as in French. The elder lady's travelling
experience consisted of a fortnight's honey-
moon in Paris years and years before. Miss
Ivory had never so much as set foot out of her
own island, and although she by no means
lacked the usual accomplishments of a young
lady, ' French of Paris ' was to her unknown.
Scant need, however, of interpreter have those
drawn towards each other by instinctive
liking and sympathy. Mrs. de Robert listened,
smiled and acquiesced, understanding as well
as could be what all this eloquence was about,
and her monosyllabic replies amply sufficed
to set the new-comer at his ease. He saw
plainly enough that his appearance was very
welcome. His kinswoman, so morose to his
predecessors, was now positively radiant. She
felt, indeed, that she had hardly anything left
to wish for. The genteel young man had
appeared in the very nick of time. The
thumbscrewing Jesuit, the men with seven
wives apiece, and the cheese-paring old maids
should not carry off all the spoil after all.

Eugenia's feelings were of a wholly different order. The notion of the least injustice being done to the other claimants was very painful to her. She did not wish the strangers to be benefited at the expense of the rest. But such surprises were very pleasant. A French-speaking guest was a novelty, decidedly an adventure; and to Miss Ivory, as to the most of her sex, an agreeable exterior and a fascinating manner in the other are ever welcome.

The 'genteel young man' of Mrs. de Robert's aspirations proved, of course, a myth. We must be satisfied always to have one half of our expectations realized, and let the other go. The new-comer was certainly not young, and not quite what old-fashioned folks would call genteel. He had passed the Dantesque half-way of existence anyhow, and perhaps might never see his fortieth birthday again. His appearance, moreover, was that of a man whose days have been spent in hardship and adventure. There was almost the look of a soldier about him, so sunburnt his complexion, so weather-beaten his appearance. The cloak,

too, that hung about his shoulders had a
military look. And the cloak as well as the
rest of his garments were well worn even to
shabbiness. He was evidently one of those
men who have scant leisure to confabulate
with his tailor. But the air of distinction,
the inborn dignity, the charm of amiable
character betrayed themselves through these
lendings. After a highly animated speech, evidently introductory and apologetic, and every
syllable of which the ladies had to guess at,
he turned to look for his travelling companion.
This was a boy of about ten, apparently of
pure Arab blood, and with a beautiful Biblical
face. Just such engaging little Ishmaels—
only in a state of nudity—the traveller meets
with who ventures beyond the Gallicized circle
of Algeria. The child, in spite of his Bedouin
antecedents, looked gentle enough, and in
his red fez and nondescript costume, half-
cosmopolitan, half-Oriental, made a charming
tableau in the hall. As to the servants, they
stood gaping at the little fellow as if he were
some wild animal of unknown species.

Meantime the conclave in the breakfast-parlour had broken up in great confusion. Mr. Meridian dismissed the claimants, first reassuring them as to the consequences of this event. He should adhere to his own division of the property—that is to say, of the available property—through thick and through thin. If the works of art, the antiquities, and the jewels had vanished, fortunately the money remained; and the money equitably divided would be theirs.

Mr. Meridian then introduced himself in the stiff literary French he was master of, and matters greatly simplified themselves. The new-comer thereupon took courage, tried to speak English—broke down laughingly, tried again; finally, all went as smoothly as possible.

'I am really an Englishman,' he said, advancing towards Mrs. de Robert, and without the least hesitation or apology kissing her on either cheek.

Next he moved towards Miss Ivory, and seemed about to embrace her after French

30—2

fashion also ; but her blush and deprecating smile made him draw back.

'Is not this, then, my kinswoman too?' he said, fascinated by the beautiful apparition— apparition indeed it seemed.

There was much more than mere feminine witchery about Miss Ivory. Nature had not only superabundantly endowed her with out- ward charm, grace, and spirit. The qualities of the heart were there also, and far outshone these.; so much rarer are naturalness, trans- parence crystal-clear, and affectionate enthu- siasm, than dark eyes, a complexion of pearl, and features with which critics can find no fault.

'Your relation ?' bluntly retorted Mrs. de Robert. 'Not she, and none the worse for that. And now, pray tell us all about this little Ishmael with eyes like blackberries.'

'This little fellow,' replied the new-comer, gathering rather the drift than the literal meaning of her speech—'this poor child'— and so saying, he patted him encouragingly on the head—'is my son——'

'I'll never believe it!' cried Mrs. de Robert, staring at the boy. 'He's brown as Joseph and his brethren, and your own eyes blue as willow-pattern china.'

'My son—by adoption,' he replied, again divining rather than understanding the drift of the interruption. 'I must tell you his history, and my own too. First let me present my offerings from sunny Africa.' •

Then he bustled about with the boy, and produced a variety of gifts for grace, use, and degustation—a carpet bright and variegated as an Algerian meadow in April, a semi-transparent cream-coloured shawl made to set off the beauty of the dark-eyed Mauresque, gay earthen vessels absolutely novel to these untravelled eyes, and appetizing baskets of bananas, olives, dates, and figs.

'Deary me!' ejaculated Mrs. de Robert; 'very good of you to spend all this money on me, I am sure; I only hope you could well spare it. However, I've always heard that these things are dirt-cheap in foreign parts—that's one comfort. Well, little darkie, let's

make a clearance, and then we'll go to dinner
—if we've got any dinner in all this commotion.'

Mr. Meridian, although pressed to stay,
now took his leave. The servants bustled
about. The visitor and his young companion
were conducted to the best bedchamber. The
Algerian gifts were made a show of in the
drawing-room. Then the little party sat
down to the one-o'clock dinner, all in airy
mood.

Now such is the contrariety of human
nature, that Mrs. de Robert would have
welcomed this Benjamin, this prodigal son
of claimants under any circumstances. The
genial, handsome stranger—for handsome he
was, in spite of his somewhat worn and
weather-beaten appearance—might have been
ungainly as Æsop and ugly as Socrates.
Her heart would have warmed to him all the
same. She had not wanted the others, that
was the plain truth of it ; but this one she did
want, if for no better reason, because he had

not come before. And, so at least she per-
suaded herself, he possessed the true de Robert
physiognomy; he was the very image of her
darling Affie.

When she discovered that his name was
Alfred, too, her delight knew no bounds. An
heir who was at the same time a namesake,
the very acme of her husband's wishes ! As
the new-comer gaily carved the chickens,
and at the same time told his story, she
sat gazing on him with a look of fascination.

'It is by the barest chance that I am
here,' he said, helping himself with a pocket-
dictionary. 'Who could have supposed that
an army-surgeon stationed on the very borders
of the Sahara, living among Bedouins and
French soldiers, should have heard of something
to his advantage awaiting him in England ! At
home, I should say, being English. Sufficient
to say now that my name is plain Alfred
Robert, the *de* having been dropped since my
grandfather, a Protestant, settled in France.

So here I am, by profession an army-surgeon, native of beautiful, unhappy Algeria, the land of flowers, sunshine, famine, earthquake, and assassination.'

'Algery!' cried Mrs. de Robert, dropping her knife and fork. 'That is the country I should like to see above every other.'

'Nothing easier,' cried her newly-found kinsman enthusiastically, and looking at Eugenia; 'I will convoy you thither. Make my bachelor quarters your own. I am now stationed in a spot that can only be described as an earthly paradise.'

'Famine, assassination and earthquakes are hardly attractive,' said Miss Ivory.

'Things are better now. I am alluding to the past,' continued Monsieur Robert. 'These miseries pass and leave no trace behind. See how light-hearted, how gay I am; yet I have had to keep my fast also. I have seen people dying of hunger around me. That poor boy yonder is one of the thousands whom the last great famine orphaned.'

'So you fathered him?' Mrs. de Robert said. 'I felt sure you were a kind-hearted creature. But go on.'

'The place I am describing lies on the border of the vast plateaux that divide flowery Algeria from the pathless desert. Remote although it be, a stray English tourist occasionally finds his way thither; from one of these I learned that inquiries were being made .for me at home. I am a naturalized Frenchman, and I love my adopted country; England seems my home, for all that.'

'We'll go to Algery with him, that we will,' Mrs. de Robert said. 'But don't let me interrupt.'

'It was no easy matter for me to absent myself. Time pressed. Official leave of absence had to be obtained, a substitute found; but all these difficulties were at last overcome, and here I am.'

'What made you bring that poor little thing with you?' asked Mrs. de Robert, looking at the child.

The army-surgeon reddened like a girl, and
for a moment showed painful embarrassment.
He turned over the pages of his dictionary in
search of a word, began to speak, faltered;
then summoning courage, got out in the same
intelligible French-English :

'I must candidly confess that I brought
the child as a living argument on behalf of
my cause. I do not need money for myself.
My wants are few, and for these the modest
emoluments of my profession suffice. I am,
however, covetous for my orphans. This is
not the only one I have adopted, and it is on
their account I cross the sea.'

' I was in hopes you had a wife and a young
family of your own,' Mrs. de Robert said,
rather taken aback; 'but all in good time.
We'll find him an English wife, won't we,
Ivey ?'

Nothing, indeed, could damp Mrs. de
Robert's ardour just then. The last piece of
information was somewhat disconcerting. A
colony of little Arabs seemed almost as ob-

jectionable, in the light of heirs, as Jesuits and
Mormons; but this charming Affie would
marry an English girl, and then make everything right.

CHAPTER XIV.

CLERICAL MOONLIGHTERS.

JUST when the festivity at Hopedale Manor had reached its acme, a curious scene was taking place at the Vicarage.

Mr. Meridian, of course, did not dance. He looked in just as the guests were arriving, and promised to return in time for the banquet. Then, accompanied by the Priest only, and provided with a latch-key, he went back to his deserted Vicarage. Such an entertainment was of too rare occurrence in the quiet village to be missed; so very considerately he had permitted his household to share the diversions of the evening. 'Nobody need return,' he said, ' till he should give the word of command.'

As the pair passed down the village street they found every house dark, and not a soul astir. The fact was, everyone had gone to look at the dancing. Ball-dresses, wax-lights, garlands, made a fairy-like spectacle to un-accustomed eyes. The band, too, of itself afforded a treat of the first water. The night. was warm to sultriness, every door and win-dow stood open; and as waltz, quadrille and mazurka succeeded each other, the inspiriting strains reached the village.

That lively music jarred on the Vicar's nerves just then. His usual flow of conversa-tion stopped. Admirably as the Priest's com-panionship suited him, sympathetic and genial as they ever found each other, to-night Mr. Meridian was absent and almost morose.

Was it the sight of Miss Ivory as she joined in the dance that disconcerted him? She wore pearls in her dark hair and round her slender throat; pearly, too, the rich white silk ball-dress, well becoming her spirited, unusual

beauty.   As she flashed past in the waltz,
now with the witty American, now with the
vivacious stranger, he began to feel vaguely
that she was wholly lost to him.

The gas throughout the Vicarage was low,
and silence reigned everywhere.   A furtive
peeper watching these two silent figures as
they noiselessly stole upstairs, might have
supposed them bent on some nefarious or
uncanny errand.   The Vicar, although in his
own house, seemed to realize the necessity of
wariness.   The Priest hardly looked at ease.

They reached the landing-place; then Mr.
Meridian lighted a night-candle, and, opening
a door, bade his companion note the number
of steps before him.

' I am taking you to a part of the Vicarage
unused in my time, or only devoted to the
stowage of lumber,' he said.   ' Yet these
nurseries are the most commodious and plea-
santest rooms in the house.'

A passage was now crossed, a second door
opened, and the host invited his guest to
enter.

An ejaculation of wonder and delight escaped the lips of the Priest ; he stood on the threshold, enraptured at the dazzling scene so suddenly revealed to him.

'Will you come inside?' said the Vicar. 'There is nobody in the house, but, under the circumstances, we cannot exercise too much caution.'

The Priest obeyed ; the Vicar locked the door from within, and the survey began.

The gas was now fully turned on, and the room blazed with light on every side. Rare and beautiful objects met the eye. The beholder was suddenly spirited away to a palace of art.

Choice pictures covered the walls, antique silver shone resplendent, gems flashed, armour gleamed ; whilst at the farther end of the room, bright, rosy, golden, as if painted but yesterday, hung a lovely, an inimitable Murillo.

'Being somewhat pressed for time, we had better take each object as it comes,' Mr. Meridian said, brief and business-like. 'Here, then, we have before us the entire de Robert collection, worth, without the Murillo, several thousand pounds. You will see that there is a little, a very little of everything, but that little of first-rate quality. The heirlooms proper—in other words, that portion of the collection really handed down from one de Robert to another, is of very inferior interest or value.'

Thus saying, he led his visitor to a stand of old-fashioned plate, engraved with the family crest and motto ; handsome and massy it certainly was, but of a kind to use, not look at. There were the much-talked-of silver candlesticks, at which the Priest looked longingly, the flower-basket of chaste design, and much else, all deeply interesting to a dealer in bric-à-brac.

'Strange how comparatively worthless is splendour without individuality, wealth un-emphasized,' said the Vicar. 'Melt down yonder service to-morrow, and you would get your precise equivalent in hard cash. But throw this into your melting-pot, and you lose something for ever.'

Thus saying, he took up a tiny silver casket, having a graceful design in relief on the sides and lid. It was a veritable gem of the silversmith's art—a trifle, but a trifle the great Cellini might have owned to without shame.

'There speaks the true artist,' he said, as he laid it down and they passed on, the Priest keenly anxious to get to the Murillo. Mr. Meridian, however, insisted on seeing everything in its proper order.

'These two pieces of tapestry,' he said, 'evidently formed part of a series illustrating the exploits of some mediæval freebooter. For what small mercies have we to be thankful in matters of history! The respectable folks, if any existed, have slipped through our fingers altogether. The historian, the artist, the poet, immortalize the villainous or the reckless! I should give these tapestries a Flemish origin, would not you?'

'In all probability it is so,' the Priest replied absently.

'We have here some beautiful specimens of old French faïence; to my thinking, one of the

most charming and satisfying of the arts.
Painters and sculptors wrought for the temple,
the palace; the potter brings art to the
home. Look at this bit of early Limoges, an
imperishable nosegay in porcelain. These
roses and lilies, modelled perhaps when a
Valois reigned in France, may outlive all the
dynasties of Europe.'

The Priest was too hurried to comment on
this sentiment.

'We have more time at our disposal than
you imagine,' Mr. Meridian said; 'pray do
not be in too great haste. The armour well
deserves inspection; it is the most interesting
of the family relics.'

He drew back a few steps in order to take a
better view.

'I fear we moderns, for the most part—I for
one, certainly—should cut but a poor figure in
these accoutrements. The weight is enormous.
There was some difficulty about the matter, or
I should have had it weighed. Of course a
fighting man in those days was a mere animal,
strong as an ox, and perhaps hardly more

intelligent. In our own time we must be content, I suppose, to read the reviews, keep apace with the Spencerian philosophy, and not trouble our heads whether we are provided with muscle or no.'

His companion just paused a moment before the armour, and that was all. The Murillo at the bottom of the room attracted him as a candle attracts the moth.

'I . do not know why jewellery always exercises such a fascination over the mind,' Mr. Meridian said, now stopping before a little case of jewels. He could easily have answered such a question for himself, had he tried. 'Is it because jewels are inseparably associated with what everybody hears of and nobody sees, Court pageants, world-famous beauties, and the like ? All of us have heard of Cleopatra's pearl ; how few ever gaze on a Cleopatra ?'

As he spoke, his eyes dwelt wistfully on a superb ruby pendant with antique setting ; it shone conspicuous amid minor gems—matchless rose in a garden-plot. The stones were of rare brilliance and purity.

31—2

'Yes, a very beautiful ornament indeed,' the Priest said carelessly, and moved a step forward. Only a case of quaint old snuff-boxes now stood between him and the Murillo.

But Mr. Meridian gazed and gazed like one under a spell. His companion called attention to this object and that; he did not so much as hear the remarks. The Priest edged on, and finally moved in front of the Murillo. The Vicar did not stir.

That resplendent jewel, globe of richest crimson light, suggested thoughts of Miss Ivory. Just as the ruby outshone its neighbouring gems, so, to his thinking, did she shine supreme among women. And the one seemed made for the other. To him, the very thought of anyone else wearing the ruby pendant was intolerable. Beautiful as she looked to-night in her white satin dress, with its simple garniture of pearls, he was longing to see her exchange this pale radiance for the more sumptuous adornment of crimson velvet and rubies. He was saying to himself that if ever any woman could look a born queen, meet for a Sebastian di Piombo to portray, it would be Miss Ivory thus arrayed. The longer and more steadfastly he gazed on the jewel the more fixed became this idea. Miss Ivory and no one else must possess and wear it. He fancied he saw her before him, and conjured up the vision so intensely, that at last it grew bewildering. For a moment he was transported with a lover's ecstasy.

The Priest also fell into a transport, but of wholly different kind. No sooner did he behold the Madonna of his dreams, the Madonna so familiar, although now gazed on for the first time, than he fell on his knees in the rapt attitude of prayer. This beautiful altar-piece made the place a veritable church to him. Outsiders might cavil at the action, colder worshippers resent the mood, but both indicated genuine religious feeling on his part. It was feeling of mixed kind. He was suddenly recalled to bygone days, and the rapture of the novitiate. He was also reminded of present needs and aspirations, rather of the Church's needs and aspirations represented in his own person.

By Divine favour that altar-piece should be his and his only ; it must not fall into mundane hands.

He was offering up a prayer, therefore, to his Madonna in heaven for the possession of this earthly semblance. Alike religious fervour and personal motives impelled him to such appeal. Passionately as the Vicar longed to see the ruby pendant set off Miss Ivory's beauty, with equal fervour the Priest craved the picture for his Sovereign Lady and Holy Mother, the Church. If the one was actuated by earthly love of exalted kind, the other's yearnings were at least free from worldly taint. Both for a brief moment clutched at an ideal, both breathed the atmosphere of a far-off, intangible world ; both became oblivious of self and of all that is comprehended in the word. The Priest was lost in silent prayer. The Vicar's mood was almost as reverential.

'I think we had better go now,' at length

Mr. Meridian said suddenly, recalled to realities. 'It is long past midnight. A fine picture, is it not?' he added, as they turned their backs on the Murillo. 'You may, of course, consider it yours.'

CHAPTER XV.

BACCHANALIAN.

VERY different was the behaviour of Mr. Bacchus. Whilst Mr. Meridian kept away as much as possible from the festive scene, Mr. Bacchus entered heart and soul into the gaieties of the evening. He realized, as well as the Vicar, all that the fête indicated—a general break-up of this pleasant little society, a sudden calm after feverish excitement—Miss Ivory's departure. And after Miss Ivory's departure, the deluge—in other words, flatness, no sort of interest hanging about anything, gloom, and despair. Under the circumstances, the lights, the music, the joyous bustle of the ballroom were not only distasteful, they were odious to Mr. Meridian. But for civility's sake, he would have preferred to remain away altogether.

The Curate, on the contrary, assumed a gala mood with the rest. He said to himself that if all happiness and enjoyment were to be denied him on the morrow, it was the best possible reason for quaffing both to the last drop to-day. He compared himself to a bankrupt; the creditors will take ruthless possession of goods and chattels next day. Till they come, was the Curate's motto, let me fancy myself a solvent man. Let me imagine the plate, the wine, the lackeys mine still.

Mr. Meridian, on the contrary, behaved like some wretch condemned to lifelong imprisonment. Away with flowers, music, and woman's smile, was his creed. Away with all that reminds me of a world never more to be my own. Let me prepare myself as best I can for the life in death to which I shall awake to-morrow.

' After all,' Mr. Bacchus said, as he drew on his gloves, about to lead Miss Ivory through the quadrille, ' my mind is quite made up about one thing. The most enviable condition in life is that of a nobody, an out-and-out nonentity. Were I Archbishop of Canterbury at this moment, I should be ready to hang myself.'

' And why ?' asked Eugenia.

' Because I could not dance with you, of course ! How very little there is you can do when you get to the top of the social tree—in the way of innocent enjoyment, I mean ! Now, just because I am a half-starved curate, I can follow the bent of my inclinations, waltz, act in " Box and Cox," run bicycle races ; in fact, I am just as independent as if the whole world belonged to me. I don't know how you feel about these matters, but I would not act as Plenipotentiary to China, or even Hairdresser to the Queen, for anything. The responsibilities attached to such positions must be maddening. Responsibility reduced to a minimum—ah! that is my ideal, the summum bonum of earthly felicity, to my thinking.'

'How happy you would be if you could get through life without a head on your shoulders!' laughed Miss Ivory.

'And without a heart in my bosom! Rid me of that incubus, and I'll put up with the inconveniences of the other,' said the poor Curate in ecstasy, one moment reduced to despondency, the next ready to laugh and cry in a breath.

He realized the hopelessness of his passion. He knew as well as Eugenia could have told him that the dignities of Plenipotentiary to China or Hairdresser to the Queen were easier of attainment than her hand. But he could not help dwelling on his infatuation, being proud of it, delighting even in the torment it gave him.

'I don't think jelly-fish are interesting,' Miss Ivory said. 'Depend on it, you are best as you are.'

If love-making could make a woman happy, Miss Ivory got enough of it that night. The suitors, one and all, felt that their last chance of speaking out had come. Not only was she on the point of disappearing from Hopedale— in other words, from the ken of both Vicar and Curate; the Transatlantic wooers saw before them a parting still more hopeless. Neither Miss Ivory nor Mrs. de Robert seemed drawn towards Columbia. They talked of visiting Switzerland, the Rhine, Italy—Bongo; but never by any chance mentioned the Kentucky Caves or Niagara.

The expression 'Transatlantic wooers' may well be used, seeing that the nephew's court-ship was chiefly done by the uncle. The epigrammatic Doctor was not only proud, but shy. He wanted Eugenia to understand exactly how matters stood with him; at the same time, he wished to spare her the humilia-tion of having in her turn to humiliate. He said to himself that there were more ways than one of letting a woman know you want to marry her; that if, for reasons best known to herself, she has nothing to say to you, 'tis only a nincompoop who cannot find it out.

Nevertheless, the wisest resolves are oft-times shaken in unexpected fashion. The Doctor was no more insensible than any other mortal to the witchery of music, roses, and the dance. Miss Ivory's appearance, too, coupled with these, seemed more captivating · than ever. Surely homage would be legitimate and timely just then.

Throughout the evening he had kept a sharp look-out on the movements of his uncle. He knew well enough that all one man can say on another's behalf would be said by his advocate, if opportunity offered. He might reason—expostulate—nothing could prevent the elder Derrober from pleading his nephew's forlorn cause. Forlorn it was, without doubt; yet under these festive influences, he grew animated and hopeful.

'Did you observe me whilst you were deep in confabulation with that ancient harum-

scarum, that venerable giddy-pate yonder?'
he asked of Miss Ivory. They were about to
dance a mazurka together, and awaited the
striking up of the band.

Eugenia looked conscious.

' Were you not taking part in the quadrille ?
I fancy you had Miss Prudence Perfect for
partner.'

' Right, so far; and at what distance,
measured by the yard-measure, do you pre-
sume I might be from you whilst so en-
gaged ?'

' Really I have no idea,' she said, smiling.

' Well, these details matter little. Con-
sidering that the band was playing all the
while, and that the rest of the dancers were
laughing and talking, as well as my partner
and myself, I could not, of course, have heard
a syllable of your discourse had you both
shouted like town-criers. I know every word
my beloved old curmudgeon whispered in
your ear, for all that ; aye, and what is more,
every word you uttered by way of reply !'

'You could make a fortune, then, as a walking telephone,' Eugenia replied jestingly, although ill at ease.

She did not feel in the least afraid of poor Mr. Bacchus. The Doctor, as well as Mr. Meridian, made her timid, apprehensive.

'I will show you twenty ways of making a fortune. Show me one of enjoying it!' cried the Doctor; 'but now for a sample of my divining powers.'

'Why repeat what you say we both know already?' said Eugenia.

'I know that I know. I want to convince you of the fact,' was the reply. 'I warrant it, the first point my respected uncle tried to impress upon you was the amiable character of his nephew. Did he not say, or make a tantamount assertion, that there was not another fellow like him for tenderness of heart, scrupulous delicacy of feeling, devotion, and so forth and so forth? Don't believe a word of it. 'Tis all Brummagem, hocus-pocus and fiddle-de-dee. Then the old gentleman

goes on to gild his gingerbread a little thicker.
" Speak of his heart, madam ! I might go on
praising it till I burst — I might indeed.
Gold is not the word for it. We must discover a purer metal. But when you come to
his parts, his mental qualities, there you
have me—I am about as much of an orator as
a donkey in ecstasies over a bed of thistles.
Look you, madam, this man is a pearl cast on
the dunghill of society. Why is he not
glorious, in everybody's mouth, hand and glove
with grandees, a figure at Court in velvet and
silk stockings ?—just because wit is no longer
at a premium in this dull world. Society
can get on without it. Were Plato now
living, he would have to higgle and haggle
for his bread like any penny-a-liner. Shake-
speare would never be asked out to dinner.
Lord Bacon himself would not find a pub-
lisher. My nephew, now—he——" but why
repeat the dear old gentleman's words ? We
can all be as fluent as Cicero about anything
we want to get rid of. I assure you, on my

word of honour, that my uncle is dreaming.
There is not a particle of veracity in what he
says. He is all froth and imagination. If
there exists a poor creature, a man who has
not a good word to say on his own behalf, that
man's name is Franklin Derrober.'

'You do not flatter yourself,' Eugenia said,
hardly knowing whether to be sad or merry.

'Do not jump with such haste at conclu•
sions,' continued the Doctor. 'The poorest
creature that ever lived may have a redeeming
quality, a flash of compensatory insight.' He
looked at her earnestly, and continued, in a
voice full of deep meaning : 'Were I to go
on my own way to the end, smug, serene,
self-confident, never allowing myself to be
carried an inch to the right or the left, either by
love—or any other folly—I might justifiably
indulge in self-contempt. But to aspire after
an ideal unreachable as the moon—to part with
one's peace of mind, with ambition and all
realities for the sake of a dream ! Yes, you
must admit there is virtue here. A man is

at least a degree above a worm who woos the .
impossible——'

'You are romancing, too,' Eugenia said,
smiling, yet sad. 'Such ideals, such dreams
have to do with great deeds, not with
happiness in the power of any woman to
give.'

'Contradict me as much as you please;
what does it all matter? Confess, when we
come to realities, you have not so much as
a crumb to bestow on the starving robin at
your window, much less a whole loaf for the
tattered beggar at your door.'

'And that may be no fault of mine,' Miss
Ivory said, softly and sorrowfully. This
strange scene was making her feel contrite
and unhappy.

'Answer me one question,' he said quickly.
'At least one starving robin, one tattered
beggar, is no more to you than another. Your
heart is free?'

She laughed somewhat bitterly.

'The heart—the heart!' she cried. 'Is

. everything in life decided by feeling? Who is entirely free ?'

She was thinking of Mr. Meridian, and of the claims he had upon her. Before the Doctor could put in a word, there he stood! The signal for supper was given. The Vicar now recalled her promise of accepting his arm. She could dance all the evening with the rest. The least she could do was to give him her company now.

' We will resume our conversation at some future time. To-morrow—or in Paradise,' the Doctor said jestingly, as she turned away with Mr. Meridian.

The Vicar, Eugenia thought, looked care-worn, even haggard ; all the more so by comparison with his neighbours. Opposite to them now sat Mrs. de Robert, squired, as she called it, by her French nephew, the new-comer from the borders of the African desert. Whilst the sunburnt army-surgeon was all geniality, insouciance and light-heartedness, his hostess beamed with exultation. The old

lady was triumphant as a maiden beside her
affianced lover.   Her cheeks were flushed with
pleasure.   She was for the moment all smiles
and good-humour.   This young man—thus she
persisted in calling him, although he was
hardly younger than Dr. Derrober—this French
nephew—here her language was equally hyper-
bolic, his relationship being as remote as that
of her Transatlantic kinsmen—in fact she might
almost as well have called Mr. Meridian a
nephew—seemed to have charmed away all
acerbity and waspishness.   There she sat close
to him, devouring every look, hanging on every
word.   'Her own darling Affie to the life,' she
murmured to herself again and again ; and
what was more, recognised as a darling in his
lifetime.

It was not only the stranger's pleasant looks
and supposed likeness to her husband that
fascinated her ; his conversation flowed in a
bright, joyous stream, and all that he said
interested.   Then he called her aunt in French,
and gracefully and endearingly acted the part
of a son ; now wrapping a shawl about her

shoulders, now pressing her to eat of this dish or that, now helping her in the duties of hostess.

'I'll tell you what it is, Affie dear,' she said, in an undertone ; 'we'll go back with you to Algery.' Glancing slily at Miss Ivory, she went on : 'That dear girl and I sadly want to visit foreign parts, and we have no one to take us. We'll pack our trunks—no great affair that— and off we'll start with you, no matter what anyone chooses to say.'

The last remark was accompanied with a malicious look at the unconscious Vicar.

Mr. Meridian was far from concerning himself with Mrs. de Robert and her new guest at that moment. He sat by Eugenia's side, mute and self-absorbed, making hopeless efforts to break from the spell that bound him.

'You eat nothing,' she said reproachfully.

'I always regard ballroom suppers as a premium put upon the seductive pastime of dancing ; or—shall I say ?—a penalty incurred by devotees of frivolity,' he replied. 'However, I will willingly give myself a week's

indigestion for the sake of gratifying you ;'
whereupon he helped himself from the first
dish that stood handy.

'What have you been about all the evening?'
asked Miss Ivory.

'You have grown delightfully inquisitive
concerning my movements all on a sudden,' he
replied, yielding to the fascination of the
hour.

He thought he had never seen her so
adorable, and his admiration, as near akin to
worship as was possible in such a nature, betrayed itself but too well.

'Is it to be wondered at just now ?' Eugenia
asked. 'You are the Sphinx, the oracle,
whose utterances we are waiting for in breathless uncertainty.'

'I wish there was any uncertainty about
the utterances of another Sphinx,' he said.
Then, anxious to avoid personalities, though
burning with impatience to speak out, he
made a great effort, and talked brilliantly and
amusingly for half an hour.

But she saw through the veil, and no

declaration of sentiment, however impassioned, could have moved her more than this stern piece of self-mastery. Even in little things he wished to be considerate, and considerateness in little things is the touchstone of a fine nature.

CHAPTER XVI.

UNTANGLING THE THREADS.

THAT festive evening was pregnant with consequences.

'My mind is quite made up, Eugenio,' Mrs. de Robert said next day. 'We'll be off in post-haste to Algery, and nobody shall say us nay. 'Tis a sweet pretty place, as I have always heard say, and Affie will be there to protect us from Bedouin assassins. You'll go, wont you?'

Whither, indeed, would not Miss Ivory go just then? For her, too, the plot had thickened; the threads of Fate were becoming more distractingly entangled than ever.

Algeria enticed from the distance as a harbour of refuge.

'We'll be off before my first twinge of lumbago,' Mrs. de Robert said, much as if the first twinge of lumbago were a fixed date in the almanac ; 'and we needn't stay if we don't like it, you know. We can come back on the day for leaving off winter flannels.' That event, according to Mrs. de Robert's thinking, seemed also marked in the calendar.

'It will be very pleasant,' replied Eugenia musingly. 'Pleasant, too, the feeling that everything is settled at last.'

'And settled my own way, not Mr. Meridian's,' chuckled Mrs. de Robert. 'He is not going to turn the four sails of my mill, I can tell him.'

Eugenia looked reproachful, as she always did when Mrs. de Robert broached revolutionary theories of this kind.

'Too late to interfere now, Roberta. You must not act unhandsomely at the last moment.'

'If a thousand pounds isn't handsome, what is—what is, I should like to know ?' Mrs.

de Robert said, emphasizing the repetition.
' They shall have a thousand pounds apiece—
I mean the old ladies, and the missionary, and
the Americans—and Affie the rest.   He is sure
to marry some day, a handsome young man
like that ; there may be a real heir to the
property after all, and my poor darling will at
last rest in his grave.'

' In my opinion,' Miss Ivory said, ' it would
be much better to leave the matter to Mr.
Meridian.   He will act fairly, and whatever
happens you need not then reproach yourself.
And you can give your genteel young man
what you like afterwards.   You are always
saying that you have no legatees but cats
and dogs.'

' I don't want to come to blows with the
Vicar.   Disagreeable as he can be, he has
saved me no end of trouble.   But what can
he have to find fault with in my plan ?   Isn't
a thousand pounds worth crossing the water
for ?   They'll be pleased enough, depend on
it !'

' But Mr. Meridian had your full authority

to act from the beginning, and is pledged now to an equal subdivision.'

'I'll tell you what it is, then, Ivey,' she added. ' If you pack off with Affie and myself to Algery, I don't care a straw about the rest. And they won't get the Murilly and the silver basket and the old china—that's one comfort.' She chuckled over the thought. 'How these things disappeared is a mystery to me. Do put on your hat, and hear what the Vicar has to say about the business. And pray tell him that we are off this day week.'

Miss Ivory looked as if the errand were not exactly to her taste just then. She also had something to say to Mr. Meridian, and wanted to get it over. But she hardly felt in the humour to have a tooth drawn at that moment.

'The sooner all this is settled the better,' Mrs. de Robert added persuasively. ' We cannot be too brisk about starting. If we put it off, a dozen more folks may come after the money. And, if not, something else is sure to prevent us from starting at the eleventh hour. No, Ivey, we won't wait a month, nor a fortnight, nor even ten days. We'll start on our travels this day week. So do go and see the Vicar at once.'

Miss Ivory realized the force of these arguments. Yes, the sooner present uncertainties were ended, and imbroglios cleared up, the better for all. She set off to the Vicarage at once.

Mr. Meridian received his visitor in the charming study that might well have reconciled some men to bachelorhood. Without and within, all was pleasantness and repose. The room was tastefully, almost coquettishly furnished, and opened on to a little rose-garden, quietude itself but for the notes of birds.

Pleasantness and repose, as far as circumstances were concerned, had certainly fallen to the Vicar's share. Unruffled by vulgar anxieties or mundane cares, born to an easy, a dignified and congenial position, endowed with moral and intellectual gifts that command respect, if they do not readily inspire affection —a supremely happy man might Mr. Meridian have been, but for one drawback. He hungered after Eugenia's appreciation, and the more he hungered the farther it seemed off.

'Mrs. de Robert asked me to call upon you,' she began ; and as she spoke she looked at her host searchingly. ' She wants to know if you see any chance of recovering the lost property ?'

Mr. Meridian's face was absolutely unreadable as he made curt reply : ' None whatever. Let Mrs. de Robert make her mind perfectly easy on that score.'

Eugenia was a deep young lady, but her insight was tempered by discretion. Seeing that the Vicar was determined to be uncommunicative, she passed on to another subject.

'Mrs. de Robert seems quite decided to go back with her latest visitor to Algeria. She would like to start in a week's time.'

' Pray tell her that the affairs she has entrusted to me shall present no obstacle. I distribute the money formally to-morrow. The twenty thousand pounds will be divided into six equal shares, and distributed amongst

her next of kin—so-called. Nothing then
need prevent a general departure.'

He spoke with feigned indifference, affecting
to hide the shock her news had given him.
Inwardly he was shaken to the very depths of
his nature. It was very difficult for him to veil
his real mood, and in jest and satire appeared
the only means of escape.

'You may realize your fondest aspirations
and get to Bongo after all, then,' he said.
'How could I be so cruel as to laugh these
bright visions to scorn ! But now you will
have your revenge. You will ride on a camel
in mid Africa, whilst I sit mewed up at home
writing sermons for clodhoppers to go to sleep
over.'

'We intend to return in the spring,' she
said, in a voice of meek apology. Every word
he had just uttered came as a stinging reproach.

'Ah,' he replied, 'take my advice, and
having once turned your back upon Hopedale,
never dream of coming this way again as long
as you live ; you have no idea how insupport-

able we should all appear to you! The very
holly-trees would be odious because they are
not palms, and even the poor sheep would give
offence because they are not gazelles. I know
how it is with you travelled folk.'

'Travel is not generally supposed to soften
people's brains,' Eugenia retorted, with much
temper. Why — oh, why was not Mr.
Meridian amiable?

'But what is ten times worse, it hardens
their hearts,' he continued, in the same strain
of light yet cutting banter. 'Nothing like a
trip up the Nile to render your next-door
neighbours insufferable; whilst a voyage
round the world has been known to turn the
mildest into critics sour as vinegar. You see,
we are such very poor creatures; but it is not
till our friends sharpen their wits by travel
that they find it out.'

Eugenia could but feel that there was some
truth at the bottom of this raillery. She
knew as well as the Vicar could tell her that
she should not return to Hopedale precisely
the same Eugenia who went away. Things

would appear different to her. Her judgments, and as a natural consequence her likings and antipathies, would be modified. She might appreciate Mr. Meridian's good qualities all the more after a temporary separation. What seemed likelier far was that new life, new influences, new modes of thought, might estrange her from the Vicar altogether.

She, too, as well as Mrs. de Robert, was conscious of the stranger's fascination. The foreign atmosphere he had introduced, the new ideas and standards of thought suggested by his conversation, his Gallic gaiety and openness of mind, were very engaging. For the first time in her existence she had come in contact with a temperament directly the reverse of our own insular sedateness and reserve.

The gay, yet much-tried army-surgeon, whose hopefulness and vivacity the severest ordeals could not check, was no mere adventurer, living morally as well as materially from hand to mouth. He was wedded to a duty arduous and ill-remunerated as can well fall to the share of any son of Adam—his very journey to England had been prompted by humanity and self-abnegation. All this had touched her imagination.

Whilst Mr. Meridian was speaking, she secretly acknowledged that his arrows struck home. What were her words worth when she reiterated intentions and promises of returning? Yet she felt compelled to say something on her own behalf.

'If I thought that a winter in the South would make me despise my old friends, I should stay at home,' she said almost bluntly.

'Would you really do that?' he asked, with a burst of passionate earnestness. Then, recalled to a sense of realities, feeling that the talked-of departure was at last no mere jest, but a hard, cruel reality, and that perhaps for the last time they sat face to face in friendly confabulation, he could resist temptation no longer. The impulse to speak out mastered him. 'Ah!' he cried, and for a moment he was a prey to feminine weakness and trembled from head to foot, whilst his voice was thick with tears. 'It is my very life that you take with you when you go away, and you will never understand.'

'But I do understand,' Eugenia replied, in tones almost as passionate as his own. 'And because I understand, I came to say something on my own account to you now. If my friendship is worth anything, if it can make you happy, take that—and for once and for all bid me not go to Algeria.'

He understood exactly the meaning of this little speech—a more magnanimous utterance surely never passed any woman's lips. She expressed her willingness to become his wife, simply because he loved her and was unhappy. The bright hopes that beckoned, the unfulfilled romance of girlhood, the dreams and aspirations not in his own power to realize—she would renounce all these if he

willed it. The motives that prompted her
self-devotion he understood also.

Recalling their intercourse during the last
few months, he saw how easily a sensitive
nature might find matter for contrition.
There was that unfortunate imbroglio with Mr.
Bacchus to begin with; and not only on one,
on a dozen occasions she had accepted his
services—services that might well seem to
claim a reward. For himself, he had never
reproached her except for not loving him.

Touched, humiliated, transported by the
magnitude of the sacrifice, he stood irreso-
lute. Now, he said to himself that he could
make this girl happy, that in refusing to
accept her self-renunciation he was yielding
to morbid scruples. Vanished a few bright
years, dispelled a few radiant dreams, and
this brilliant Eugenia would need sure an-
chorage as any common woman! What
was the worth and stability of these toys,
these gewgaws, she now clutched at so
feverishly? Travel, adventure, romance, for-

sooth! would she be any the better or happier for them in the end ?

Might not the existence and love he offered give surer guarantees of happiness than any glimpses of a more varied life, any stranger's fancy? For himself, he could speak with assurance ; for others, he dared not answer.

These thoughts flashed through his mind swift as lightning. For one wild moment, the crowning joy of life seemed his own. He saw his home made perpetually sweet and beautiful by her presence. He stood on a pinnacle of earthly bliss, the envier of none, envied by not a few.

But the bewildering vision would not stay. Clear, unanswerable justice made itself heard, and swayed the storm of passion.

He drew back horrified at the bare thought of yielding to such a temptation. Even with the most rigid exercise of self-control and toleration on both sides, would such a compact be endurable? A wife's devotion without a wife's tenderness! oh no! better, a thousand times, loneliness and isolation than the inevitable retribution of loveless wedlock. She was proud as well as himself. Her unhappiness would ever be studiously veiled from his ken, that he knew right well. But unhappiness must be the final portion of both.

Of no colourless nature this bright, beautiful Eugenia; she was born to expand as a rose in sunshine. To accept the gift of her life on such unequal terms seemed, now that the scales had fallen from his eyes, little short of sacrilege.

All these thoughts were come and gone in a few moments. Swiftly as if the decision had been instantaneous he answered her.

'If my love is worth anything, is it not capable of some sacrifice also?' he said, wholly broken down, for once using the language of real tenderness.

'Go to Algeria,' he added. 'Go anywhere you please. Forget Hopedale altogether. Only be happy.'

Her eyes were full of tears, and he, too,

could not get out another word. They shook hands in tearful silence; then she passed out of the carol window into the garden, and thence, without being observed, by a field-path to the Manor.

CHAPTER XVII.

O Sabina and Prue had come into their great fortune at last! They were able to sit down and inform old friends and neighbours at home, that they had really heard of something to their advantage. They wept, they giggled, they knelt down and solemnly thanked Heaven; they lay awake till dawn, making plans for the future; finally, both succumbed to the overjoy. They took to their beds, from which it required all the Curate's medical skill and philosophy to raise them. He exhorted, reproved, and sermonized—prescribed pills, powders, tonics, and sedatives by turns; and after a day or two his specifics worked the cure. The pair rose one morning, feeling said Sabina, as if nothing had happened after all.

' And after all, nothing has happened worth mentioning,' continued the little woman, endeavouring, as usual, to shake off earthly dross. ' You and I get several thousand pounds apiece, which merely means so much more money henceforth paid to butchers, grocers, drapers, and undertakers; for of course we must die some day, and our end will be considerably hastened by living on the fat of the land. There cannot be two opinions as to that. Now, had you written a second Waverley novel, and jumped into world-wide celebrity—had I discovered that I could sing like Jenny Lind, or dance like Fanny Elssler—we should have had something serious to crow about.'

' We must crow about what we have got,' Prue replied cheerfully; 'and how many much more deserving than ourselves would be thankful to have as good cause. I still feel, I am sure, as if I were standing on my head.'

'I assure you, now that the first surprise is over, I feel as if the matter were not worth a second thought,' Sabina said, with an air of superiority. 'Of course, had my Edwin been by to share this good fortune with me, things would now wear a wholly different aspect. I am to-day, at heart, as I was twenty-five years ago, a sorrowing widow.'

'A sorrowing widow is better able to support her troubles when she has a little money in her pocket,' Prue said. 'After the struggles we have had to make ends meet and keep up a respectable appearance on eighty pounds a year between us, we ought to rejoice in being able to set up our carriage—well, not that exactly, but a pony-chaise will certainly be within our means, and between walking and riding is all the difference in the world. Then there are the poor to think of. How pleasant to feel able to bestow money as well as tracts and good advice! The poor people at home always seemed as grateful as possible, I must say that for them; but when you can give half a pound of meat to a hungry man, it's more to the purpose.'

Sabina tossed her head.

'You will, of course, do as you choose with your own. For my part, I never mean to lay out a single farthing on charity, so-called. My endeavour will be to improve the tastes of the working-classes by offering prizes for poetical compositions, and paying the learned to lecture to them on the philosophy of the Stoics. My Edwin was always talking about them—Zeno especially.'

'Would that sort of thing be generally understood?' asked Prue doubtfully.

'It doesn't do to give people what they understand, as Edwin used to say. I remember his words so well. "Bina," he said—"Bina, if you want to elevate your fellows, discourse to them on something quite beyond their comprehension. That is the secret of all great intellectual revolutions."'

Prue still looked discommending. These

theories savoured to her of irreligiousness.
Sabina, to her thinking, always stood on the
brink of Stoicism, or something equally dreadful. Poor Prue often wished Edwin's wise
saws at the bottom of the sea. They worried
her extremely.

Thus, then, chatted, in spite of Sabina's
deprecations, the happiest pair of mortals
under the sun. Sabina had a well-thumbed
copy of Johnson's 'Vanity of Human Wishes'
in her pocket, and produced it from time to
time, in order, as she expressed it, to keep
down ebullitions. 'Let us be as happy as
the day is long,' Edwin used to say; 'but for
Heaven's sake, no ebullitions.'

In the midst of their lively talk the door
was opened an inch, and Prue caught sight of
the Curate. He was beckoning her out. She
was with him in a moment. He invited her
into his study, and, standing with his back
to the window, said in a husky voice :

'I am feeling very unwell—have got a
splitting headache—and this sermon, by hook

or by crook, must be finished to-night.
Do you think you could possibly do it for
me ?'

'I will try,' Prue said, inwardly trembling.
She had no literary experience whatever, but
would never have dreamed of refusing the
Curate anything.   Had he asked her not only
to write the sermon, but to stand up in the
pulpit next morning and preach it, she would
have said 'Yes,' to oblige him.

'It is not at all a difficult subject,' continued Mr. Bacchus — 'about Ruth and
Orpah; and the text is, "Whither thou goest,
I will go, . . where thou diest, will I die, and
there will I be buried." You have but to
resume the thread of my discourse.   All is as
straight sailing as possible.'

'I can but do my best,' replied Prue, smiling.

'Best or worst, it will be a sermon all the
same, and I dare say much better than my
own generally are.   So scribble away,' said
the Curate.

He closed the door, and Prue heard him go upstairs to his bedroom and lock himself in.

' What could there have happened ?' wondered Prue. ' He spoke of headache, but his disordered looks betokened mental rather than bodily distress. Was it some pecuniary difficulty he had got into ?—some claim put in that he had no means of discharging ?' She thanked Heaven that it was now in her power to relieve him of such anxieties. Nothing could repay his kindness to Sabina and herself, and Mr. Bacchus was the first who ought to benefit by their improved fortunes.

Then she dipped pen in ink, and valiantly scribbled away. If there existed an avocation in which Prudence Perfect was born to shine, it was certainly that of writing sermons. She had the Scriptures at her fingers'-ends, and although without any apprenticeship to the sublime art of scribbledom, could write sweet, unalloyed, rustic English.

But it was not of literary skill she thought

now. Sabina had spoken of Jenny Lind and
Fanny Elssler. Prue's raptures might rather
be compared to those of Sappho in her most
impassioned mood, or of Jeanne d'Arc when
first hearing the heavenly voices. The task
before her seemed in itself sacred; the fact of
Mr. Bacchus having set it, lent additional
sweetness and solemnity. She felt that, no
matter her want of learning, her incapacity,
her inexperience, she must make her words to
live. The subject, too, exactly suited her
frame of mind. Was she not like Ruth in
Bible story? Did she not feel that whither
the Curate went, she must go; and where he
died, there must she be buried? Tears of
mingled ecstasy and sorrow rose to her eyes,
but she dashed them away for the sake of her
work. Mr. Bacchus was in the habit of
making his sermons long. 'Poor people,' he
used to say, 'liked to get as much as possible
for their money. They would listen to him
all day, if he chose to hold forth.'

So Prue's pen moved as if she were

under the spell of inspiration. She knew
exactly what form the composition of a sermon
should take—a piece of knowledge not astonishing in one who had listened regularly to two
on Sundays and as many on week-days as she
could get at for well-nigh thirty years. The
orthodox division into heads was now strictly
adhered to, the stereotyped parallels brought
into relief, the historic coincidences dwelt
upon. . Then came the general summary and
the moral, and here Prue was little likely to
be at a loss either. She was a first-rate
moralizer. If anyone could extract a moral
from a dumpling, it was Prue; and if the
homeliest subjects could thus be turned to
account, what might one not expect when she
took in hand a theme so lovely and suggestive
as that of Ruth and Naomi ?

Fluent as she had been on the subject of
Moab and the genealogy of Obed's son, she
excelled herself in retelling the story of a
woman tender and devoted as herself. Her
whole being thrilled with emotion whilst

penning the last page. Not only the delight
of being serviceable to her friend and the
conviction of a hitherto undiscovered gift im-
parted a glow of satisfaction ; she felt supreme
pleasure in thus being set on a level with
Christ's ministers, for once perhaps being
made instrumental in leading the thoughtless
to heaven.

She had just accomplished her task, and
was glancing at her manuscript with silent
rapture, when the Curate burst in.

'You don't mean to say you have done
already ?' he asked, with a look of relief. 'I
only wish I could be half as expeditious. But
you are new to the business. You would
find it as tiresome as I do after a while.'

'I hope it will do. Have you time to look
through it ?' asked Prue nervously.

'Oh,' said Mr. Bacchus, 'I have time
enough for anything. It is the head I want.
I assure you I could not read your sermon
just now if you paid me twenty pounds.'

This somewhat ungracious remark would

have damped Prue's ardour, but for the Curate's look of extreme wretchedness. There was a wild expression in his eyes, too, which frightened her.

She put aside her manuscript sadly. The sweet meed of praise she had expected from his lips was not to be her reward as yet.

'Oh!' she said, 'something very serious, I am sure, is the matter. Will you not tell me what it is?'

The poor Curate threw himself on the sofa, and burst into tears.

'You know already,' he got out. 'She is going away next week—Miss Ivory, I mean.'

'Do not be so cast down. Sooner or later she will come back again,' Prue said, ready to weep, in her turn, out of compassion.

That sweet, artless voice of comfort but made the Curate's tears fall faster. There he lay sobbing, the very personification of helplessness, misery, and despair.

'She will never come back,' he murmured. 'I foresee exactly what will happen. She

will marry that Frenchman! Why was not
I born a Frenchman?'

Prue had risen to go. She felt a delicacy
in staying. He would naturally like to have
his grief to himself. Divining her intention,
however, the Curate stopped her.

'Don't forsake me, dear,' he said, holding
out one hand and motioning her to sit down
beside him.

Prue, blushing and smiling through her
tears, did as she was bidden. Still grasping
her hand, he went on :

'I assure you, if it were not for the poor
children and kind friends like yourself, and
for the look of the thing, being in holy orders,
I should make away with myself. It was as
much as I could do to keep from jumping
into the horse-pond just now.'

'Oh!' Prue cried ; 'you would not thus
destroy your valuable life! And think of the
misery you would cause others!'

'I don't want to make others miserable.
I know what it is too well myself,' Mr.

Bacchus went on. 'My life henceforth will be as uninteresting as if spent within the four walls of a prison. A man must be very far gone to feel like that.'

'Great griefs pass, under God's blessing,' Prue said, mildly persuasive. 'You may be ready to jump into the horse-pond to-day, but this day twelve months you will very likely feel as cheerful as possible.'

'Then if that day ever comes,' the Curate replied, more fully realizing the sweetness of Prue's sympathy every moment—'if that day ever comes, will you marry me?'

'Oh, thank you!' Prue said, wholly over-come. 'Thank you very, very much.'

'What you have to thank me for, I can't conceive,' bluntly retorted the Curate. 'If you were not forbearance itself, you would be ready to trample me underfoot like a noisome reptile. I ought not to have mentioned this, of course, till the time comes that I do feel cheerful. But if I ever do again, will you now—will you really marry me?'

34—2

' Of course,' whispered Prue.

' Of course ! I see no of course in the case,'
again broke in the self - reproachful Mr.
Bacchus. ' You are a rich woman now, and
I haven't a sixpence. How I have the impudence to ask you, I can't imagine. I am
always doing things I can't imagine I should
do, were I driven to it.'

' But, fortunately, other people see us in a
different and more favourable light than we
do ourselves,' Prue said, all appreciation and
tenderness.

' I am thankful you see me in a favourable
light. It is the one ray of sunshine in gloom
black as night. I hope I shall feel better
when the dreadful day is over, that is all. I
am sure it will be as bad to me to see Miss
Ivory steam off by train with that Frenchman
as to take part in her funeral.'

' It will not be so bad for her. When we
love our friends very much, we must rejoice
in their happiness, whether we can share it
with them or no.'

'I wish I could feel so,' retorted Mr. Bacchus. ' But I am not a good Christian— never was. I cannot bear to have my fondest hopes dashed to the ground ; yet if they had been realized, if Miss Ivory had married me, such happiness would have been my soul's destruction. I see that written on the wall.'

To a woman less oblivious of self than. Prue, these outpourings would have been anything but flattering. As sweetest flattery, however, she accepted every word. Was he not confiding in her because she was to be his wife ? The wild fancy for Miss Ivory, she said, would pass away. Her memory would gradually become to him as a beautiful dream. Prue was conscious of no jealousy, no uneasiness; only a little secret satisfaction, at the thought of Miss Ivory's coming depar- ture. It was better both for the Curate's peace of mind and her own that Eugenia should go to Algeria.

' I certainly feel a trifle better,' he said,

after a time. 'Suppose you read me your sermon? If I should fall asleep you would forgive me, would you not? You know, all preaching always has a drowsy effect, more or less.'

Prue briskly took up the manuscript, and, greatly to her delight, the Curate did not go to sleep.

'On my word!' he said. 'It is A 1! You won't catch me writing many sermons when we are married, I can tell you. I only wish you could preach 'em, too. However, we need neither write nor preach sermons unless we please. The world will be before us where to choose, as to Adam and Eve. But I wish now you had not come into that money. I mean, I wish I had asked you to marry me before you did come into it. Do what I will, I cannot prevent my conduct from appearing in the most odious light. The fact is——'

But Prue would not permit him to say what the fact was. 'It is so much pleasanter to look forward than backward,' she said; 'and not all the talking in the world will prevent women like Miss Ivory from turning men's heads.   Helen of Troy could not help herself ; but, for all that, she caused a deal of mischief, poor woman !'

CHAPTER XVIII.

MORE DISENTANGLEMENTS.

MEANWHILE the prodigal son, the Benjamin of claimants, was in high favour with everyone. Nobody, except Mrs. de Roberts, had a word to say against the others; the ladies were found amiable and sympathetic; the elder Derrober all old-fashioned chivalrousness and enthusiasm, the younger ever entertaining to listen to; the Priest, besides being urbane and eloquent, was a mystification to be admired at a distance. With the last new-comer it was a case of general falling in love at first sight, and this fact may be taken as strikingly illustrative of human character and human history.

In the other men had been embodied spiritual
and intellectual activity, philosophy, faith,
speculation. The stranger personified action ;
and it is the men of action who have fascinated
the majority of their fellows from the beginning of chronicled time until now. Mrs. de
Robert, for instance, may be taken as an
average type of humanity, neither better nor
worse, neither wiser nor simpler, than the
ordinary run.

She could not help listening to the animated
talk of the first three—she really liked them in
her own heart ; but neither the discourse of
priest, philosopher nor satirist took any hold on
her imagination. She did not feel as if these
kinsmen belonged to her. Very different was
the case of the army-surgeon. His brief stir-
ring narrative of exploit and adventure she
delighted in, and could understand. To have
that dear Affie in the house, as she expressed
it, was the next best thing to consorting with
a real live Robinson Crusoe. The pathos
of his position, too, would have been irresistible even in a commonplace man. This

handsome, sunburnt, weather-worn hero had
gone through as many hairbreadth 'scapes as
Othello. Gently born and bred, circumstances
had compelled him to face the most cruel trials
that confront humanity. The sight of vast
populations decimated by hunger and un-
housed by earthquakes; defenceless villages
stormed by infuriated Arabs bent on pillage
and slaughter; fever and pestilence rampant
in the land—all these ordeals he had passed
through, yet his sunny temper and faith in
humanity remained intact. Whilst recounting
past experiences, he could all the same throw
heart and soul into this new English life,
familiar to him hitherto in novels only.

Mrs. de Robert might do her best to
monopolize the favourite of the hour. He was
here, there, and everywhere—at neighbouring
tea-tables and lawn-tennis courts—ready to
sing, waltz, play duets, help to get up a picnic.
Nothing in the way of recreation, new experience or sociability came amiss to him ; and
to crown all, in spite of being a Frenchman—
which, in popular phrase, means a scoffing

Voltaire—when Sunday came round, there he was at the parish church, with Mrs. de Robert leaning on his arm!

As for Miss Ivory, she saw less than anyone of the fascinating stranger; yet they were already on delightfully cordial terms.

'My time to enjoy your society will come in Algeria,' he said, laughingly triumphant. 'I must not rob your friends of a single quarter of an hour now. You ride, of course. I will procure for your use a gentle-tempered Arab horse. We will breathe the very air of the desert together.'

This indulgence in prospective freedom, this foretaste of new experience and adventure, was not the most attractive feature of her new life. Algeria would not be Hopedale. In Algeria, Hopedale problems would cease to perplex her. No more painful decisions impending, no more inner conflicts at hand! And the realization of her wishes so far, Bongo, or what was next to Bongo, at last—palm-groves, Bedouin tents, and the dusky population of the desert!

'For my part, when we get there, I should like to stay and become a second Lady Hester Stanhope,' Mrs. de Robert said, in high glee at the thought of setting out. 'And as to you, Ivey, I know what you'll do in the end. You'll marry that dear Affie; and those jewels, if we ever recover them, shall be yours—with more besides.'

Miss Ivory laughed away the insinuation, but Mrs. de Robert continued with the utmost gravity :

'Oh yes, laugh as much as you please. We may laugh or cry. Things work one way or another, and sometimes for the best. I feel as certain as my name is Sarah Roberts that you will marry a de Robert after all ; and if you do, I give you my word for it, I'll leave you the best part of my money.'

'I would marry a chimney-sweep on those conditions, of course,' Miss Ivory replied, with much seriousness.

'Humph !' cried Mrs. de Roberts, affronted ; 'I hope you don't compare Affie to a chimney-sweep.'

'One might as well marry a chimney-sweep as a saint, provided he is an acquaintance of only four-and-twenty hours' standing, or thereabouts. But have it all your own way. Marry me to the Dey of Tunis, if you please. We are at last to set forth, like Don Quixote and Sancho Panza, in search of adventure. I can think of nothing else.'

'I do wish we could take the poor dear cats,' sighed Mrs. de Robert. 'I cannot bear the thought that they will perhaps be low-spirited without us.'

'Foreign cookery might not agree with them, nor with the dogs either. I think they will be happier at home,' Eugenia replied.

'There is ever some drawback to happiness in this life,' Mrs. de Robert said. 'However, Affie has promised, if I am homesick, to bring me back at a moment's notice. I am tired to death of Hopedale, and all the people in it; but I dare say as soon as ever I have started I shall cry my eyes out to return. To go all the way to Algery seems a madcap scheme, at my time of life.'

'My dear Roberta!' Miss Ivory exclaimed, opening her eyes wide; 'don't you know that what seems an adventure to us, is no more to the rest of the world than a trip from London to Hampstead Heath? Sir Thomas Bates, you remember, visited Algiers and Morocco when he was verging on ninety; and . the Miss Spencers, when both past eighty, went up the Nile, and climbed to the top of the Pyramids! The older people are, nowadays, the farther they travel.'

'The more fools they, then!' was the rejoinder. 'What do old folks like myself want but our cats, warming-pan, and buttered toast? However, I'll go as I've said I'll go, Ivey, although I feel a presentiment that this journey will be the death of me.'

Miss Ivory knew her old friend's whimsicalities too well to take these observations seriously. The Algerian project would wear a dozen different aspects in Mrs. de Robert's eyes ere the moment of departure came. But the departure would take place.

The news of this romantic expedition had, of course, spread like wildfire through the place, and formed the chief topic of conversation. In more cosmopolitan circles such a scheme excites little curiosity or astonishment. To 'winter with the swallows in Algeria' nowadays is not more difficult of achievement than a trip to Brighton. But Hopedale folks travelled seldom. Wedding tours were generally made to London, or, at farthest, to Paris. Valetudinarians journeyed to Moffat or Torquay. It only rarely happened that anyone got as far as the Rhine or Chamouni.

For the most part, people kept their money in their pockets, and travelled by means of the book-club or circulating library. But to set off for the confines of the desert, and under French guidance, savoured of the marvellous. Some predicted one thing, some another; but all came to the conclusion that Miss Ivory would marry the new-comer, Alfred de Robert. It could not be otherwise.

'Talk the four sails off yonder windmill, talk Morecambe Bay into a cedar forest, talk a garrison of fools into wise men, you will never make me believe that I have a chance with Miss Ivory,' said the Doctor to his uncle. ' However, in order that you may not reproach me till my dying day, I will go this very afternoon and ask her.'

' There speaks my valiant Frank!' cried the old man, delightedly clapping his hands. 'Go in for the prize and win!'

' A fool's cap, or a woman's scorn. The wisest have discerned as much before now,' was the reply. ' Well, Mr. Curmudgeon, what am I to say?'

' Say, indeed! Say to such a girl as that? The veriest dolt that ever breathed would feel inspired at the very sight of her.'

' Say what other lovers have been moved to say under the same circumstances, from Adam downwards.'

' And more barefaced lies men have never uttered!' cried the Doctor. ' Would you have me swear that I am ready to lay down my life for her? Paltry concern as it is, she knows I would do no such thing. Shall I vow that she shall mould me to her will, that I will prove ductile as wax in her fingers? When did a man so much as change the colour or shape of his waistcoat to please his wife? Ought I to swear that I love her? A sorry jest that! The wretches who have cheated their wives, proved faithless to their wives, robbed them, beaten them, murdered them, did they not all swear once upon a time that they were over head and ears in love? No, sirrah! teach me something more to the purpose to say to Miss Ivory, or by my faith I'll stay at home!'

'You are right so far, Frank. I don't think a girl of sense and spirit wants to be harangued upon such an occasion. Make thy offer pithy; woo her with thy wit, man; let thy understanding take her heart by storm!'

'I'll tell you what it is,' Dr. Derrober said, getting up. 'I'll just say, " Eugenia Ivory, will you marry Frank Derrober?" When a man has said that, has he not said everything? What matters it whether he is ready to marry her for her beauty, her sprightliness, or her

fortune? Not a jot that I can see. The gist
of the matter lies in the fact that he is ready
to marry her at all. He can but wed one
woman, and from the millions that breathe on
this terrestrial globe—the dark-skinned, the
blonde, the clever, the gay, the queen of
society, down to the milkmaid—he has chosen
her. That is to say, he fain would choose her.
So poor as such a compliment may be in most
cases, to say nothing of my own, 'tis the best
a man has it in his power to make. Off I
am !'

'Heaven's blessing go with thee, my lad !'
ejaculated the elder fervently.

'Don't bother Heaven about my affairs
any more just yet,' quoth the irreverent
Doctor. 'Have we not got our money?—a
thousand times more than our deserts ?
Should we not now leave Heaven to do our
neighbours a good turn? Bye-bye, old gentleman. Take care of yourself in my absence.'

Thus saying, the Doctor started jauntily on
his errand. He was not the kind of man to
be cast down under any circumstances. This

something to his advantage, this solid piece of good fortune in the shape of several thousand pounds, if it could not exalt, was at least not calculated to depress. A certain stoical resignation, a secret conviction of the hopelessness of his case, made him take refuge in outward gaiety. Moreover, he could not endure the thought of causing his uncle pain.

As good luck would have it, he found Miss Ivory alone. Mrs. de Robert, with her pseudo-nephew and the little Arab boy, had driven to the nearest town in order to make purchases. Eugenia stayed at home—must it be confessed?—having urgent business with the milliner. After the usual greetings, he plunged straight to the heart of his subject.

'Is it ever worth while,' he began, 'to ask a question when we know beforehand exactly how it will be answered?'

'That depends,' replied Miss Ivory gaily, although her colour went and came. 'I suppose, in ninety-nine cases out of a hundred, we know exactly how our neighbours are. Yet with what persistence we always say

" How d'ye do?" as if they had just been dug
up after an earthquake or risen from a sick-
bed.'

'Can we ever be quite positive, for all that,
how a question will be answered?' continued
the Doctor. 'It seems that, alike in the
weightiest as well as the most trivial cases,
there must ever be a margin of uncertainty.
For instance, I once asked a veritable skin-
flint, a money-grubber, to lend me a hundred
pounds. I felt it was just as likely that Mont
Blanc would turn on a sudden to barley-sugar.
The incomparable niggard actually said " Yes."
There is also this point to consider. Are
there not manifold questions that never ought
to be propounded at all, by their intrinsic
delicacy shut off from speculation, relegated
to perpetual doubt, silence, and obscurity?'

'Certainly,' Miss Ivory replied, still animated, but uneasy. 'What so impertinent as
to connect a slate-pencil with the doings of
the soul hereafter, mahogany tables and im-
mortality?'

'I fear that I now put myself into the category of mahogany tables and the slate-pencil,' resumed the wooer, outwardly playful, although in an earnest mood.

'Miss Ivory, one jest before we part. Pray, madam, why do you put on this missyish air of innocence when you know as well as I do that Frank Derrober has a heart? " What if he has?" say you. " Small concern of mine. I've hearts enough and to spare, handy, if I want any." Aye, madam; but, an it please ye, 'tis very much my concern. Well, I grant you, a heart is a poor thing in itself; but for all that 'tis a man's microcosm, his stock-in-trade as an immortal, the pack containing his all-in-all as he wanders a pedlar through the world. Am I and my wares just nothing to you?— so much Brummagem?'

'What can I say?' said Eugenia, taken by surprise, although she had tried to prepare herself for such a disclosure. She liked this genial, witty, insouciant Doctor. She could not bear the notion of paining and disappointing him. But there her feelings for him began and ended.

'What can you say ?' he asked, determined to
keep up his spirits to the end, to do battle for
himself bravely, but, if worsted, to bear defeat
with a cheerful air.   'Frank Derrober,' he had
said to himself, 'no ordinary tussle this.   Fight
with tooth and nail, lad ! fight while any
breath is left in thy body ; for remember, if
sent sprawling on the grass now, vanquished
ignominiously, 'twill be thy first, last appearance in these lists.   No more fray on account
of ladies' smiles ; thy last hope of shining in
such a tourney vanished for ever!'

'What can you say?' he repeated.   'I am
the very person to come to in your quandary
—the prompter with book open at the right
place.   Say, then, "Does a more impudent
fellow exist on the face of the earth?   But
softly; there is a grain of honesty in his composition.   Many of his sex, I'll answer for it,
can hardly boast of that; and candour is the
best of soaps.   It washes the conscience clean.
As he has told me the worst himself, there will
surely be no pitfalls for me to stumble into.
Again, a potent argument in his favour, he has

strolled half-way down the garden of life without so much as coveting a single rose till now. If not sweetest flattery this, at least evidence of nice judgment and fine taste on his part." '

' You think much too highly of my poor self,' Miss Ivory said, anxious to stop him, not quite knowing how.

' Madam, you are but as God made you. Small credit to Eugenia Ivory for being what she is. She could not alter the colour of her eyes or cut down her stature by an inch, if she tried till Doomsday. But perhaps I have not your ladyship's permission to prompt you further ?'

Miss Ivory, making an effort to be quite self-composed, did now put in a deprecatory word.

' I am very sorry——' she began.

He sprang to his feet in a moment, hat in hand.

' Now I bow to my sovereign lady, and accept dismissal. Pretty words these, but none have ever caused more cruel pangs. The editorial " I am very sorry "—how many

garreteers has it driven to suicide? The
official "I am very sorry"—is it not the
epitaph of buried ambitions too numerous to
count? Your "very sorry" I will believe,
though, truth to tell, I seldom believe anything. Who but children and idiots do? I
wish you well then, madam, although you
have dealt me a nasty blow. Plasters and
poultices won't heal it. 'Twill hurt me all my
life; 'twill accompany me to my grave. But
I hope you will be happy. You are as innocent of these villainies as a baby that puts
its little foot into the cream-noggin. Farewell.'

'We shall meet again. You are not going
to leave Hopedale before us?' she said, feeling
bound to say something.

His raillery disconcerted her more than any
mere display of feeling could have done. The
underlying bitterness was but too apparent.

'Only stay here till the crack of doom, or as
near it as possible, and we stay too,' he replied. 'But we understand that a precursory,
a lesser crack of doom, is to take place one

day next week.   In other words, Miss Ivory
quits Hopedale.'

' Yes, Mrs. de Robert is going to start with
me for Algeria,' she said, blushing, she hardly
knew why ; leaving out all allusion to her
companion—she hardly knew why either.

He added, in the same tones :

' Under the circumstances, you would be no
farther off at Timbuctoo or in the moon, and
no nearer if we were to remain perpetually
next-door neighbours.   Only be happy, wherever you are !'

' I hope you will be happy too !' she stam-
mered forth.

' I promise not to jump into the Falls of
Niagara, or blow my brains out with a re-
volver.   Will that satisfy you ?'

Then he took his leave, and on reaching
home, so well dissembled his chagrin that the
elder Derrober secretly consoled himself.

' Thank God !' he reflected ; ' this wound is
not incurable after all.   My poor dear Frank
will pull himself together and marry, in time,
some pretty countrywoman.   And, thanks to

decidedly the most disagreeable old woman it
was ever my luck to come in contact with—
whom may Heaven crown with felicity!—we
have at least something to pop into the pot
without thinking beforehand, and a roof to
shelter us both as long as we live. It is
astonishing how a golden windfall will turn
white hairs brown again, and soothe all cares,
even disappointed love!'

CHAPTER XIX.

AT THE RAILWAY STATION.

SO the precursory crack of doom had come at last.

Early one bright September morning the little railway-station at which Sabina and Prue had alighted a few weeks back showed unusual signs of animation. One by one hither flocked Miss Ivory's friends and lovers to bid her God-speed and farewell. The ladies had flowers in their hands. A magnificent bouquet of exotics ready for presentation to Mrs. de Robert might be seen in the waiting-room. As the hour of departure drew near, all faces were turned anxiously towards the Hopedale road. Even the station-master and porters shared the general curiosity.

'Oh dear!' said Mr. Bacchus—he had changed his mind at the last moment, and joined the rest—'I do trust nothing is the matter—that they won't be too late, I mean. It would be quite shocking to make us go through the same trial again, just for all the world like a rope that snaps at a hanging!'

This not over-chivalrous speech was addressed to his future wife, but Prue affected to take it as a matter of course.

'I dare say Miss Ivory feels as I do, and will not come till the last moment. Saying good-bye is as bad as having a tooth out—to affectionate people, I mean. It can't be got over too quickly.'

'After all,' put in Sabina, whose mind at such moments as these was ever full of the lost Edwin, 'as Edwin used to say—I remember his dear, wise words so well—" Never bluster or fluster, Bina," he said. " We are never really too late for anything—so long as we are alive, of course. If we miss one train, we can take the next. What we can't do to-day we can most likely do to-morrow, or ten years hence. Too late," he used to say, " is a fiction, except in the mouth of a fish-salesman." '

' Or plethoric spider letting his brisk neighbour gulp down unwary flies,' put in the Doctor, who had just come up with his uncle. ' Ladies, I hope that you feel all the better for having this little business settled at last. We are now—Heaven be praised!—worth being robbed and murdered; as I take it, the true criterion of gentility, the just ambition of every well-regulated mind.'

Prue glanced at her lover, and smiled.

' I don't think such terrors disturb us much,' she replied.

' And thieves and murderers don't tell us when to expect them, like duns and bailiffs,' put in Mr. Bacchus, with a grimace. ' We are not in a perpetual misery of expectation.'

' My feeling is that we ought to present our esteemed friend the Vicar with a testimonial,' said the elder Derrober. ' But for him, I feel

sure of it, we should never have got a half-
penny. Here we were, and here we must have
stayed, subsisting on public charity, a charge
to the parish.'

'I am ready to meet the most exalted views
on the subject,' put in the Doctor, with a hand
in each pocket, rattling what coin he chanced
to find there. 'Unless I soon rid myself of
my superfluous wealth, I feel that blood-letting,
or some other desperate remedy, will be necessary. But here comes the old harridan—I
mean our esteemed benefactress—with Miss
Ivory, the juvenile Mahomet, and the Frenchman; and post-haste behind, cheek by jowl,
the two parsons.'

The elder Derrober glanced anxiously at his
nephew. How could he bear this trying
ordeal? The Doctor, however, had schooled
himself into self-possession. He looked care-
worn, like a man whose nights have been
troubled; but throughout the scene remained
every inch himself—animated, swift of speech,
as if this were one of the happiest moments
of his life.

Prue, too, glances uneasily at the Curate. He was all excitement. His eyes shone, his pale cheeks were flushed; he looked like a man under the influence of some unwholesome stimulant.

'Thank God, it will soon be over!' he said to himself, as Miss Ivory, beautiful and radiant, drove up.

Not that Eugenia could leave her friends and lovers without a pang. This series of farewells was painful to her as well as to them; but the tension of the last few weeks had ended. She was free! At the approach of the pony-carriage there ensued a little commotion. The porters ran up to load themselves with wraps and umbrellas. The Doctor, all alertness, helped out the ladies before their French visitor could dismount. The elder Derrober gave Mrs. de Robert his arm. Mr. Bacchus volunteered to take the tickets, and, of course, took them for Liverpool instead of London. Sabina and Prue bustled into the waiting-room after the bouquet. The Vicar and the Priest, who arrived a minute after, chatted in French with the army-surgeon. The Doctor kept close to Miss Ivory.

'I so hoped that the train had gone without us !' ejaculated Mrs. de Robert. 'I feel every bit as if you were all bundling me into a hearse.'

'At any rate, you don't look like it, my dear madam,' Mr. Derrober said, smiling. ' Permit me to say, even, that you appear the picture of health ; and long may you live to enjoy the satisfaction of making six people happy !'

' 'Tis little enough you have to thank me for,' jerked out Mrs. de Roberts. 'But, bless us and save us, what on earth is this ?'

Seeing that time pressed, and that everybody else was occupied, Sabina and Prue now produced the presentation bouquet. It was a veritable triumph of the florist's skill—a real work of art, possessing but one drawback. It could not be preserved, and it could not be eaten. That sheaf of blush-roses, Neapolitan violets, and maidenhair fern was ephemeral

as ice-palaces constructed in Northern capitals
—a marvel to-day, nothingness to-morrow.
Appended to the bouquet was a more solid
offering in the shape of a small silver drink-
ing-cup, on which were engraved the initials
of Mrs. de Robert and some of her grateful
next of kin.

'We all wanted to show our appreciation of
your kindness,' began Prue, no longer timid
as of old.

It was astonishing how the fact of Mr.
Bacchus's declaration, coupled with that of
her good fortune, had given her self-con-
fidence. She did not dread her awful kinswoman now any more than the Curate's baby.

'You couldn't have laid out your money
worse,' blurted forth Mrs. de Robert. 'I was
never fond of flowers squeezed together like
herrings in a barrel. And what will it look
like when it gets to London, I should like to
know?'

A week ago such a rebuff would have completely disconcerted both Sabina and Prue.
To-day, however, they were both too much

exalted by their altered circumstances to care
a straw what Mrs. de Robert chose to say to
them.

Prue went on persuasively :

' We understood that you were going to stay
a few days in London, and have brought a
basket for the flowers.   They will look bright
on your dinner-table.'

' Much time shall we have to look at them !'
was the ungracious reply.   'And what's that
gimcrack dangling below ?'

'That is a small goblet for travelling pur-
poses,' Prue continued, with as much composure as before.

Just then the Priest came up.

' You will observe, my dear cousin,' he said
blandly, addressing himself to Mrs. de Robert,
' that the names of the donors are but five.
We Jesuits bestow upon the poor only.'

'Quite right too,' replied Mrs. de Robert.
' However,' she added, turning to the others,
' I thank you, all the same ; and the bouquet
shall go with us to London, since we have no
carriage to pay for it.   How late the train is,

to be sure ! I wish, for one, that it would not come at all. I never repented of anything half so much in all my life as of this wild-goose chase to Algery. Not one of us will ever see Hopedale again—that I feel certain of.'

Meantime, chance had favoured the lovers so far. Alike the Vicar, the Curate, and the Doctor got a parting word with Miss Ivory. Each had kept a sharp look-out for his opportunity, and made the very most of it when it came.

The first to be thus favoured was Mr. Bacchus. Impetuous as a schoolboy, he had proffered to take the tickets ; blundered as to the destination ; finally, come back triumphant and apologetic.

'There you are!' he cried, as he handed Miss Ivory the tickets and the change. He glanced round, and seeing that no one was by, added in an eager undertone : 'I feel as upset by your departure as if I had fallen from the top of a church-steeple. But you won't be bothered with my importunities any more.

I am going to marry again.' He glanced at the distant figure of Prue, and went on : 'No choice lay open to me. I was ready to hang myself when I heard that you were really going off to Algiers. And when I have a wife I shall be obliged to put a stop to such desperate thoughts.'

'I hope you will both be very happy,' Eugenia said.

She felt sure that it must be Prue of whom he was speaking. He looked crestfallen and ashamed.

'I don't deserve her. I don't deserve the love of any woman,' he whispered. 'You have made a fool of me till the end of my days.'

Just then a porter came up with a sovereign of Eugenia's money that the agitated Curate had left on the counter. That little incident created a diversion. Mr. Bacchus returned to the ticket-office to assure himself, as he said, that he had not left his head there !

Meantime, very alertly the Doctor took his place by Miss Ivory's side.

'What a comfort to me to feel that I have been perfectly useless to you,' he began— 'never rendered you the tiniest personal service whatever! Think of me as of some poor little struggling moon in the human universe, content to have been illuminated by its sun for one brief moment, then to sink back into perpetual darkness.'

Was he in jest or earnest? Miss Ivory hardly knew. She was but a girl. There are many things that books cannot teach us, and this is one. What may a naïve maiden know of a man's passion? Yet some glimmer of the truth seemed to reach her—something like conviction seemed to flash across her mind. She looked at him with a tender entreaty for pardon in her true eyes, and replied tremblingly :

'Forgive me for not being other than I am.'

There was no time for him to say more. The Priest now came up to take courteous leave ; then he made way for Mr. Meridian.

The Vicar was calmness itself, but rigid ; it was as if he feared to speak lest this painfully attained self-mastery should play him false at the last. When he spoke, his voice was strained and unlike his own.

'You will let me hear from you occasionally,' he said, in that tone of authority he could hardly help using even towards her. 'I shall want to know your plans.'

'Of course I will write. We intend to return to Hopedale in the spring,' she said.

But the cheering words had no meaning for his ears. His face had a blank look. He was on the verge of losing presence of mind.

Now, indeed, the white clouds of the coming train could be distinctly seen through the trees. Mr. Meridian's lips trembled, his eyes filled with tears.

'What would I not give to be going with you!' he said; and the words were as pathetic as those of a sick man when he sees robust companions setting out for a holiday excursion.

Eugenia's eyes grew moist also, and she pulled down her veil as he conducted her to the railway carriage.

Then followed a chorus of farewells, good wishes, and ' God bless yous.' Sabina and Prue were finally overcome with emotion. The Priest wiped his eyes. Even Mrs. de Robert looked ready to cry as she sat holding Mr. Affie's hand.

' Don't forget to go and see the poor cats !' she shouted to Mr. Meridian, as at last the train steamed out of the station ; the army-surgeon waving his cap and reiterating :

' Au revoir ! au revoir !'

Mr. Meridian turned drily towards the little group on the platform.

' Now that Mrs. de Robert is fairly off,' he said, with an odd expression, ' I may as well tell you that you are all richer than you imagine. The much-talked-of treasure — the pictures, the plate, and the rest of the de Robert heirlooms — certainly vanished ; but the thief was myself. I saw as plainly as a man can see anything that drastic measures were necessary. I was driven to some such expedient by the necessities of the case.

Suppose you all come to the Vicarage this
afternoon and inspect your new property ?'

There was a clamour of thanks, but the
Vicar did not stop to say more.   Inviting
his companion to be seated, he stepped into
the pony-carriage, and drove off, only looking
back to say :

'Won't you come too, Bacchus ?'

So the train having Miss Ivory for pas-
senger steamed off in the direction of London,
and on three hearts left behind there settled
a gloom most of us can understand.   Who
has not lived through a similar experience ?
Over the beautiful world broods the very
genius of peace.   The blue heavens are not
more dazzlingly fair than the green flowery
earth.   But that curl of white smoke disappearing through the trees means for us all the
emptiness and bitter sense of loss that any
human heart can feel.   The wheels of life
move on briskly as ever.   The bustle of busy
multitudes drowns our sighs.   Gradually we,
too, learn to smile again as we take our usual
places at the board of life, though with scant

appetite and in no humour for saying grace. All that made life's summer vanished with that speeding train.

Mr. Bacchus would forget and be happy. The Doctor was too much of a Rabelais, of an Odysseus, to break his heart.

But Mr. Meridian in his quiet Vicarage, would he ever recover the blow? Would he ever be the same again? .

.

'One thing is quite certain,' said Sabina, at the close of this eventful day. 'Edwin made me see it clearly more than thirty years ago. Oh, the wise woman I should have been had those thirty years been spent by his side in blissful wedlock! "One thing is as certain as Holy Writ. Pray, my dear Bina, implant it on your mind," he said. "The precariousness of human affairs baffles the understanding of the sagest. Newton himself could not have prognosticated what might or might not happen to a shoeblack as he walked down the street. But no matter in what sphere of life we are thrown, we are bound to keep our eyes

open.   The wise as well as the foolish may
any moment, and in most unexpected fashion,
hear of something to their advantage."'

Our little drama, then, is played out at last,
and the curtain falls, but not on certain issues
only.   Just as one romance often begins where
another leaves off, so the conclusion of a play
may suggest many an unwritten scene.   The
question of Mrs. de Robert's next of kin was
satisfactorily settled for once and for all, but
others remained of equal interest to all concerned.

Would Miss Ivory return in the spring?
Would she marry Mr. Meridian, and settle
down to the life of a clergyman's wife after
all? or, what seemed likelier far, would she
give her hand to the light-hearted but heroic
stranger who had enticed her to far-off shores?
Might not her old friends hear of her as
moving in a wholly new sphere, taking the
initiative, perhaps, playing a noble and
courageous part in some European colony
under an African sun?   She would find there
an ample field for her energies, and wide scope

for the disposal of her fortune. And the high-spirited, much-tried army-surgeon, who bore an English name, would he not rise to future eminence in the country of his adoption? Made independent by this inheritance, might he not become a foremost pioneer in colonization—a providence to many?

Thus folks speculated concerning the pair. They finally came to the conclusion that Miss Ivory would at some future time bear the name of de Robert, and thus become related by marriage to her old friend.

Mr. Meridian kept his own counsel. The questions put to him concerning the travellers he answered unsuggestively. The de Robert jewels, however, he retained in his keeping, and occasionally examined them with wistful eyes. They were destined for Eugenia. He had made up his mind all along that no other woman should wear them. Alas! he feared now that she would possess but too valid a claim. In his secret heart he never looked for the return of the wanderers.

For the present, Sabina stayed with her

friend Prue, though it seemed likely that she, too, would ere long choose a home for herself. The elder Derrober's plans of a Phalanstery pleased her. She had half promised to join in the venture, and throw in her lot with those of the speculators.

'Yes,' she would say, as she gazed on the charming landscape from the Curate's window, ''tis a sweet place; but, as Edwin used to observe, "One place is just as good as another, if we look upon the matter in a proper light. The wise man will go into raptures over a cabbage-bed as readily as over a waterfall. The one is as much of a miracle as the other, if we go to the bottom of things." '

'But we can't always go to the bottom of things,' put in Prue. 'The created world is, of course, wonderful in its most trifling detail; but it is natural to prefer gazing on a waterfall.'

'It is not good for us to be always gazing on waterfalls,' Sabina added. 'As Edwin said

—I remember his words so well—"Bina," he said, " Bina, accept the earthly and unearthly by turns. Cultivate spasms, be spasmodic, for only thus will you avoid a dead-level of feeling and perception. Put David before your mind, who danced in religious transport one moment, and the very next fell in love with his neighbour's wife. In order to keep clear of soul-killing indifference, we must let the mind get the upper hand to-day and the body to-morrow." '

Prue looked unconvinced. She could not bring herself to approve of all David's doings, any more than of all Edwin's conclusions.

'The worst of being spasmodic,' she said, ' is that we can't always stop spasms when they once begin. And, of course, David was an exception, held up more for edification than example.'

She was wondering how she should feel if her future spouse should dance in religious ecstasy one moment, and look admiringly at another curate's wife the next. No such suspicions, however, disturbed her peace of mind. She trusted the Rev. Mr. Bacchus implicitly; and trust is the corner-stone of affection.

EPILOGUE.

W ITH some of his own stories, a romancer falls in love at first sight ; with others, he becomes gradually enamoured ; for yet a third order, his feeling is steady, jog-trot friendship, which neither increases nor abates till author and dramatis personæ quietly take leave of each other at the colophon.

But from the moment that the story-teller dips pen in ink, and seeks to give his little world a local habitation and a name, to clothe his characters with flesh and blood, this is the real world to him, and the other mere nothingness and phantasmagoria. His next-door neighbours, all life, buxomness, and jollity, seem much less like substantial realities. He shuts himself up in his study, and consorts with the more tangible folks he finds there. And now comes to my mind a fable of the witty Greek writer, Lucian.

Diogenes, according to this fable, asks Hercules how, being a god, he has got to the under-world.

'Oh,' says Hercules, 'I am in heaven, sure enough. It is only my shadow, my phantom, strolling about here—not myself.'

Diogenes, not satisfied with this explanation, wants to know how Hercules can be so sure of the matter. May it not be the shade in the upper region, and the real Hercules that inhabits the dominions of Pluto? A subtle disquisition follows as to which is which, leaving the two disputants where they were when they began.

The novelist in earnest is very much in the position of Lucian's god. He inhabits two worlds, by turns being a shadow among realities, and a reality among shadows. Winning or grotesque, comely or hard-featured, stern or adorable, these fictitious personages, creations of his brain, exist for him, become, for the time being, his brethren and sisters, next of kin and near neighbours. If he succeeds in puzzling his readers, as the cynic and the god are puzzled in the fable—if, for the time being, he contrives to make the work-a-day world phantasmal and remote, and the world of his fancy near and tangible— then, .ah, then he has wielded a wand indeed; and has nothing to fear from the scorn of critics or the verdict of Time!

THE END.

BILLING & SONS, PRINTERS, GUILDFORD.

G. C. & Co.